DEATH RATTLE

ROBBIE DORMAN

Death Rattle by Robbie Dorman

www.robbiedorman.com

ISBN-13: 978-1-7336388-7-6

Cover design by Bukovero

For Izzy.

1

"Give me your money, grandpa! All of it! Now!"

Ebner Graves looked into the reflecting mirror nestled in the corner of the ATM. He stood in front of the Fleet Savings and Loan, seeing the man standing behind him, a pistol in his hand. The bottom half of his face was covered, and the small mirror distorted too much for him to get a good read. He had noticed someone loitering on the far edge of the building, but he had assumed it was just a homeless. More and more of them these days. He didn't blame them. It was hard now.

"I'm going to turn around," said Ebner. He ran his hand through his closely shorn white hair and turned, setting his lined face on the thief. He looked down on the robber, his lean 6'1" frame all sinew and gristle.

"Your cash. Now!" said the robber, the pistol only a foot away from Ebner's face. Ebner had just taken his grocery money out of the ATM, his weekly ritual disrupted. He studied the man, a hoodie pulled over his head, a bandanna covering the bottom half of his face. Ebner set his dark eyes into the robber's, brown and big, and saw them waver.

Ebner decided then this man wouldn't be getting his money.

"No," said Ebner.

"What do you mean, no?" asked the robber. "Give me your fucking money or I'll shoot you in your fucking face."

"No, you won't," said Ebner, staring past the pistol directly into the man's eyes. "You won't shoot me. Not over two hundred dollars."

"Don't tell me what I'll do, grandpa," said the thief. "The money."

Ebner sighed, rubbing his eyes. "Patrick, what are you doing?"

The mugger wavered, the gun moving left, then right. His voice bounced, doubt mixed in with the bravado. "Don't know who Patrick is."

"You think I don't know those eyes? That voice?" asked Ebner. "I ate dinner with your grandparents before you were even dreamed of. Me and Stan cracked jokes over lunch beers. I babysat your mother, held her close when she cried. I saw you at your grandpa's funeral. When did we bury him? Three years ago. You were bawling like a baby. And I don't blame you. He was a good man. We miss him, don't we?"

Patrick's voice caught in his throat, soft, a sudden halting noise, but he raised the gun again. "I need the cash. You don't understand."

"You think robbing old men in front of the bank is the best way to get it?" asked Ebner. "Cause maybe you'll get it this week or the next, but this trick won't work for very long before one of them blue boys shoot you in the street. Who will get money for your little one, then? Leave Jess to take care of him alone?"

Patrick's gaze finally broke then, looking down, his big brown eyes watery now. He looked back to Ebner.

"Stop talking and give me the money."

"Patrick, I'm not giving you my money," said Ebner, his voice dry and firm. "It's not happening. Give me your pistol."

"No," said Patrick.

"Give me your gun, or I'll take it from you. And if I have to take it from you, I *will* march you down the street to the police station myself. Do you know what the sentence for armed robbery is? You've never been to jail, have you? But it won't be jail for long. It'll be prison. And there ain't no coming back from that."

The gun moved again, losing strength, the heavy piece of steel trembling.

"Don't test me, son. My sympathy only goes so far," said Ebner. He stared hard at Patrick, waiting. Patrick's breath came heavy.

Finally, the pistol lowered out of Ebner's face, and Patrick looked down, and held it out by the barrel to Ebner. Ebner took it from Patrick's hand with practiced ease, the heavy pistol cool in his palm. He unloaded it, popping the round in the chamber into the air and then onto the ground with a soft *tink*. He ejected the clip and tucked it into his back pocket. The gun served only as a club now.

"What's the money for?" asked Ebner.

"Stevie needs special meds," said Patrick. He couldn't meet Ebner's gaze. "Without insurance, it's too much. The credit cards got rejected."

"What you been doing for work?" asked Ebner.

"Roofs, out at Sunny Meadows," said Patrick. "But it's under the table."

"Have you talked to Ted, down at the recycling center—"

"He's only hiring part-timers," said Patrick. "I can't piece together three part-time jobs into a real one."

"Talk to him tomorrow," said Ebner. "We go back. I'll have a word, see if he can't find a full-time position for you. Alright?"

"Yes, sir," said Patrick, finally looking up again.

"Go home to Jess," said Ebner. "This never happened."

"Yes, sir," said Patrick, pulling down the bandanna and flipping back his hood. He looked into Ebner's dark eyes again, just for a second. "Thank you."

Ebner nodded, and Patrick turned to leave. Ebner stopped him.

"Patrick." Patrick looked back.

"Who sold you the gun?"

The bell dinged behind Jeff Marshall. He polished the parts of a rifle. "Welcome to Marshall's Guns and Ammo, how can I help you?" he asked mindlessly.

"Why are you selling pistols to Patrick Hart?" asked Ebner, putting the pistol and the clip in front of him on the glass counter without a sound.

"Hello, Ebner," said Jeff. Jeff was in his forties, heavy around the middle, with a buzz cut. He used to serve, but he'd gotten soft without the exercise. Ebner stared at him.

"I sold him a pistol because he wanted one. It ain't rocket scienc—"

"He wants a full refund," said Ebner.

"Does he now?" asked Jeff. "Strange, I don't see him. Maybe he could come in—"

"What do you think he wanted a pistol for? That boy ain't never shot a gun in his life. He wasn't going to take it out to the range."

"It's not my responsibility to question everyone that comes in here about why they're buying what they're buying."

Ebner only stared at him. "He wants a refund."

Jeff stared back and then sighed. "He paid in cash."

"Then I'll take it back, in cash."

Jeff sighed again. "I won't ask why you're doing the asking." He walked to the register.

"Probably a good idea." Jeff popped it open. "It was $450, including the ammo. You don't got that, do you?"

"Don't worry, you'll get it back, too."

"I bet I will," said Jeff, counting out the money into his palm. He returned to Ebner and pushed out the cash. Ebner took it, quickly flipping through it and shoving it into a back pocket.

He turned to go without a second look at Jeff.

"Maybe wonder next time, Jeff. Maybe wonder why they want the pistol," said Ebner, and he left.

The late summer sun hit Ebner as he stepped outside of the gun store, and his eyes creased to narrow slits until they adjusted. The worst heat was past them.

He stopped by the recycling center next, open seven days a week, smelling like garbage and metal. Ted sat in his tiny office, the door open. He watched something on his phone.

"You got more cans, Ebner?" asked Ted.

"Naw, probably not for a couple months or so," said Ebner. "I'm here to ask about work."

"Thought you were retired," said Ted, finally looking up at Ebner.

"It ain't for me, Ted," said Ebner. "Patrick Hart."

"Yeah, I told him there was part-time work if he wanted—"

"Part-timing ain't going to help him. He needs full time."

"It ain't in the budget, Ebner," said Ted. "I can't afford to offer benefits, cuts into my bottom line."

Ebner sighed. "Don't make me do it."

"Oh, come on, Ebner, please—"

"I'll do it, I swear I will—"

"Ebner—" Ted put out a hand, trying to stop a bear with his palm.

"I'm calling in my favor," said Ebner. "Give him a job Full time. Benefits."

Ted dropped his hand and looked down. "Goddamnit." he said, under his breath. He looked up again. "Fine." The word came out like a gunshot. "But we're even now. All square. Alright?"

"Alright," said Ebner. "Have a nice day, Ted."

"Absolutely," said Ted, a sneering smile on his face.

Ebner returned to his truck. His heart felt a little lighter now, now that he could get back to his normal Sunday routine. He'd miss the first few innings of the Rangers game, but he wouldn't rush. Rushing made him forget, and he wouldn't be back into town until the next Sunday, not if he could help it.

He stopped by the feed store first, to get the bird food he liked. Said hello to Jennifer at the counter.

Next was Martin's Auto. The truck needed wiper blades and an oil change. He got the parts and said hello to Martin. Martin showed off pictures of his grandbaby.

Morris' Hardware was last before the grocery store. Before the grocery store 'cause if Morris was in—and Morris was always in—then the ice cream would melt before he got home.

Ebner drove down the main drag, his window rolled down. One more empty storefront this Sunday. The little diner that tried the spot next to the antique store couldn't stay in there. Ebner had meant to visit, but it had escaped him. Must have escaped everyone. Fleet's main drag wasn't big, but big enough, but every month that passed got emptier and emptier. Wasn't just the storefronts that were empty. He noticed more and more vacant houses, too. Fleet was drying up.

Morris waited for him, smoking a cigarette in front of his store, reclining in one of the two rocking chairs there. They were for anyone, but Morris was the one using them 95% of the time. Morris wore what he wore every day, a starched white dress shirt underneath overalls. The cigarette dangled from between his lips, and his eyes were permanently lidded against the sun, even when it wasn't shining.

"Those things will kill you, you old bastard," said Ebner, climbing down out of his truck.

"They ain't got me yet," said Morris, gesturing to the other rocking chair. Ebner considered it for a long moment and then sat down, easing his bones down onto the wood. "But you might be right."

"It's a curse," said Ebner.

"What? Being right all the time?" asked Morris.

"Yep," said Ebner. A silence settled between them, for a moment, long enough for a breeze to fly down the drag. The street was silent.

"How's business?" asked Ebner, breaking the quiet.

"Terrible," said Morris. "But you know that."

"There's always hope," said Ebner. "Maybe things will turn around."

"That's true," said Morris. "But it's pretty slim right now. Most people drive up to the Home Depot out in Walton rather than come down here. Prices are cheaper."

"But then they miss the sights," said Ebner.

"Not sure if that's a plus anymore," said Morris. Another long pause. Morris took a drag on his cigarette and blew out the smoke in a plume, the warm breeze carrying it away. "How you coping?"

A stab of pain hit Ebner in the heart, and his breath stopped, just a moment. Loud enough for Morris to hear, he was sure. That was alright.

"I'm surviving," said Ebner. "Finding ways to stay busy."

"You talk to John?" asked Morris.

"Couple times a week," said Ebner. "When I can."

Morris nodded, a motion Ebner felt more than saw. "How's he doing?"

"I don't know," said Ebner. "He doesn't say much. Feel like I have to drag the words from him."

"Now you know how it feels," said Morris.

"I talk plenty," said Ebner.

"Only took you forty years to learn," said Morris. "It was his daddy. Ain't an easy thing to lose."

"He's got the shop," said Ebner. "I know he's putting a lot of time in."

"Burying your head in work won't get you away from the grief," said Morris. "You're not an exception to that, either."

Ebner paused. "I know."

"You speak to Joanna?" asked Morris.

"Not recently," said Ebner.

"You should," said Morris.

"You know how it is between us," said Ebner. "And Will isn't here anymore to keep the peace."

"You should still talk to her," said Morris. "It'll be good for both of ya."

Another silence settled between them. Ebner could feel the routine pulling at him, the lost time at the bank, and extra trips in town.

"I need to get going," said Ebner, simply. He pushed himself from the chair, the wooden handles creaking underneath him.

"Wait," said Morris, his tired, old voice laced with a hint of urgency. Ebner froze and sunk into the chair. Ebner looked at him and cocked an eyebrow. Morris looked back, their eyes meeting for the first time today. "Has Mr. Fuchs come to talk to you yet?"

"Man who owns Sunny Meadows?" asked Ebner. "I've heard talk of him. Haven't seen him, though."

"He's been coming around," said Morris. "Handsome fella. Tall, taller than you."

"Yeah?"

"Yeah," said Morris. "He wants to buy the store."

"Your store?" asked Ebner.

"Yep," said Morris. "Made me an offer after sweet talking

me for a bit."

"How much?" asked Ebner.

"More than it's worth," said Morris. "Far as I can tell. Enough to retire on."

"What did you say?" asked Ebner.

"I told him thanks, but no thanks," said Morris.

"Sounds like a good offer," said Ebner.

"Probably is," said Morris. "But there's more than money. You know that. This place is all I've got left, aside from you. I think I'd like it to keep on going as long as I can. With the smokes, it might be less than earned, but that's alright."

"Why do you ask?" asked Ebner.

"Because he's been making offers to everyone," said Morris. "Everyone that owns their land, at least. And some people are taking 'em."

"Hard to say to no to it, way things are going," said Ebner.

"I understand," said Morris. "But way things are going, Fuchs will own the whole town."

"You can't be the only one not selling," said Ebner.

"I'm not," said Morris. "But there's a fair few. And he'll be talking to you, sooner or later. About your land."

"The woods?" asked Ebner. "It ain't good for nothing but deer."

"You kidding me?" asked Morris. "It may be full of nothing but trees and ticks, but it's the primary piece separating Sunny Meadows and Fleet proper. He'll want it."

Ebner looked out over the main drag of Fleet. A car drove by then, an old white sedan, a mismatched rear quarter panel.

"What do you think his plans are?" asked Ebner.

"I don't rightful know," said Morris. "But he ain't buying

it all up out of the kindness of his heart. He's spending that money because he knows he'll make more. And whatever's here after he gets his hands on it."

"It won't be Fleet anymore," said Ebner.

"No," said Morris. "Not the Fleet we know."

"Don't know how long it'll last anyway," said Ebner.

"Some truth to that," said Morris. "But if Fleet's gonna go out, I think I'd like a say on how it goes."

"That's what this is," said Ebner. "Whatever he makes it, it won't be Fleet anymore. It'll just be Sunny Meadows."

"That's what I reckon," said Morris.

"Yep," said Ebner. He got up, forcing his old bones out of the rocking chair. He felt a tinge of pain in his hip, but it eased as he stood up. "I'll be seeing you, Morris." He started toward his truck.

"Ebner," said Morris, that same tone of voice. Ebner looked back, caught Morris' thin eyes, wide as they get.

"I do have other errands today, Morris," said Ebner.

Morris ignored him. "You remember Lieutenant Harper?"

"Yeah, I remember him," said Ebner.

"You remember the look in his eyes, back before it?"

They had marched for a few days, and it wouldn't stop raining.

Ebner walked in front of Morris. It was the middle of the day, if it made a difference. It had rained for days on end, monsoon season, and no matter how often Ebner changed his socks, his feet were always wet. He didn't know where they were. He had looked at the maps, and tried to make heads and tails of it, but after a while he couldn't keep all the jungle in his head. Morris knew where they were, and he stuck close to him.

"Where's he taking us, Morris?" asked Ebner.

"I don't know," said Morris. "Far as I could tell, we're way off the grid." They weren't the only ones talking. Whenever they made camp, everyone whispered about Lt. Harper and the look in his eyes. You saw it in the guys who spent too much time in the bush. Who'd been out too long. Who'd lost something inside. They all were miserable, and Harper wouldn't tell them where they were going.

It had been a slow, steady descent. The targets had been of less and less tactical value. And Harper hadn't let them near the comms. They were in the dark, following him around, killing what he ordered. The squad spoke without speaking.

"He's going rogue, and he's taking us with him," whispered Morris, one night, in the dark. Morris talked to everyone.

They stopped within an hour. They had arrived at their destination. Harper gathered them off the road. Ebner knew everyone in the squad by name now, and they all looked at Harper, his wide, empty eyes glancing back and forth between them all.

"Men, we're here," he said. "A half klick up on the road. A village. They're hiding charlie. And we're going to take them out."

"Why this village?" asked Morris.

"Shut up and follow orders," said Harper. "We'll surround it, and when I give the command, open fire. Leave no one standing."

McIntyre came back then, pushing his way through the brush. "Nothing but women and children, Lieutenant."

"It's a trick," said Harper. "They're hiding them!" Ebner and Morris exchanged a glance. A glance that only lasted a moment, but told Ebner everything he needed. They'd heard the stories. They all had. And Morris talked to everyone.

"Let's get into position, men," said Harper, his gaze looking everywhere but his men's eyes. Ebner looked to the all the other men, and he saw them for what they were. Whatever was in Harper's eyes, it wasn't human anymore.

He turned, and Ebner didn't hesitate. He pulled his knife and drew it across Harper's throat, pulling it as deep as he could, pushing Harper down, who tried to hold the sudden wound closed. It did no good, and the squad watched as he died.

It rained as they dug a hole for him.

"Yeah, I remember," said Ebner.

"Same look," said Morris. "Same eyes. Something ain't right about him. You watch him close."

2

Ebner had planned to head straight home after the grocery store, but the lights were on inside his shop.

John's shop, now. It's not yours anymore.

It was a hard habit to break, after you own something for twenty years. It wasn't his anymore, but John never went in on Sundays. He'd stop in. The ice cream would keep.

He found John inside, hammering on a piece of metal fencing. Various other finished fences laid up against the walls.

"Surprised to see you here today," said Ebner, waiting for a moment of silence in between the banging. John paused with the hammer held up, and then put it aside, taking off his protective glasses. He cast a glance at Ebner. John was short and stocky, with thick black hair, cut sharp. He looked like his mother Joanna, all except his eyes. When Ebner looked into John's eyes, it was like seeing William all over again.

"I imagine someday you'll remember to knock," said John.

"You wouldn't of heard it anyway," said Ebner. "That's a lot of fence. Looking pretty good."

"Thanks," said John. "It's a big order."

"How're you doing?" asked Ebner.

"I'm doing alright," said John. "You?"

"I'm doing alright," said Ebner. "You know."

"Yep," said John. Silence filled the shop, and Ebner searched for something to say.

Mentor the kid, Ebner. He listens to you.

"I've never been good with kids, Will. You know that," said Ebner. They sat in the shop, Ebner tinkering with something. That part was fuzzy now, a thousand projects ago, but Will sat there, as handsome as he ever was, trying to talk sense into him.

"He ain't no kid anymore," said Will. "He's thirty-two, for christssakes. Jesus God, he's thirty-two."

"What am I supposed to say to him?" asked Ebner.

"Give him advice. I try and tell him what to do, and it passes right through him. You'd think *you* were his father."

"I'm not good at advice," said Ebner.

"You liar," said Will. "You do it all the time." A beat of silence that feels awkward with everyone else, but natural with Will. "They're closing the plant."

"What?" asked Ebner. He stopped tinkering. "They can't close."

"Course they can," said Will. "Just because it's always

been here doesn't mean it always will."

"What will Fleet be without it?" asked Ebner.

"I don't know," said Will. "But it's keeping John close, and without it, he'll leave."

"Would that be so bad?" asked Ebner. "He's still young."

Will sighed, and Ebner heard all the conflict in that breath, all the worry, and the fear, and the love. "I don't want him to leave. Neither does Joanna."

Ebner met Will's eyes, his green-gold eyes. "I don't neither," said Ebner. "I'll talk to him."

"Ebner?"

John's green-gold eyes looked into Ebner's. "You there?"

"Yeah," said Ebner. "Sorry. Lost in my thoughts. Happens a lot in my old age."

"Better than the alternative," said John.

"You're right about that," said Ebner. A pause.

"Anything else you wanted to talk about?" asked John. "I'm trying to get this order done before next week."

"Uh, well—" Ebner paused. "I guess I do. You heard about this fella, that's been snooping around town, making offers to people?"

"Yeah," said John, his eyes going back to the fence. "Mr. Fuchs. He came by. We talked." John's voice had changed, something else in it, something Ebner didn't like.

"What did you talk about?" asked Ebner.

"The shop. Fleet," said John. "These fences. It's his order."

A line of thoughts flashed through Ebner's mind, but his mouth outraced them all. "Did he make you an offer?"

"Of sorts," said John.

"What was it?" asked Ebner.

"He wants to buy," said John. "Said he has plans for Fleet,

and said the shop is an integral part of it. Said he would take ownership, rebrand it, but keep me on as manager."

"How much?" asked Ebner.

"A lot," said John. "High six figures."

Ebner breathed. The place wasn't worth that. The land, the equipment, everything all together wouldn't go for that on the open market.

"Seems too good to be true," said Ebner.

"That's what I thought, too," said John.

"What'd you say to him?" asked Ebner.

"I told him I'd think about it," said John. "And that I'd get back to him."

"When was this?"

"Early this week," said John. A truck passed outside, the walls rumbling.

"What are you going to tell him?" asked Ebner.

"I don't know yet," said John.

"You shouldn't sell," said Ebner. "He's not being upfront with us. Buying up property left and right. He's already got Sunny Meadows. Who knows what he's going to do with it after he's got it."

A long beat of silence. John only stared at the piece of fence he was working on.

"These fences are my first order in three months, Ebner. Three months. I've been cleaning out gutters, and hauling stumps, and emptying septic tanks just to pay the bills."

"It's honest work," said Ebner.

"But I don't want to do it," said John. "I'm a metalworker. Not a handyman. Looks like to me that Mr. Fuchs is bringing money into town, and Fleet sorely needs it. I sorely need it."

"That may be true, but what happens when he don't need you anymore?" asked Ebner.

"Then I'll leave, with all the money he's paid me," said John. "And I'll start somewhere new."

"Just leave Fleet behind, just like that?" asked Ebner. "Your mother—"

"Mom would come with me," said John. "What's left here for her?"

"I—"

"You talked me into staying here," said John. "Back when the plant closed. Hired me on. I appreciate what you did. I appreciated it then, and I appreciate it now. It kept me close to Mom and Dad, and to home. And you taught me a lot. But Fleet—Fleet is dying. Look down the street. What do you see? Empty storefronts. People who can't make their house payments standing at intersections, hoping for spare change."

"It used to be—"

"It used to be something special, I know," said John. "Dad said it all the time. Told me Fleet was *something special*. That he was proud to be from here, to raise me here. Well, Dad's gone, Ebner. And Fleet's not far behind him, unless someone does something. Maybe that someone is Mr. Fuchs."

Ebner took a breath and held it, letting it out slow. "You notice anything strange about him?" asked Ebner.

"No," said John. "He was dressed nicely. But he's a businessman. He seemed excited. Genuine. That's what I saw in his eyes."

Ebner thought to Morris' words about him. About 'Nam, and Lt. Harper. It seemed impossible they were talking about the same man, but then again, Harper's mania had been genuine.

"I don't trust him," said Ebner. "And I know that if you sell to him, you lose any say in what happens to this place."

"I stayed here because of you, Ebner," said John. "Because of what you did for me. And Mr. Fuchs is doing the same thing. He's helping Fleet by doing this."

Ebner only shook his head. Something was wrong. He knew it.

"Shake your head all you want," said John. "But it won't change anything."

"Just think it through," said Ebner. "Don't do something you'll regret."

"I haven't done anything yet," said John. "And I won't argue with you, Ebner."

"I just—I just want Fleet to be something again," said Ebner.

"So do I," said John.

"I should get home," said Ebner. "I've got ice cream melting."

"Better hurry then," said John. "Thanks for stopping, Ebner. I mean it."

Ebner thought to hug him, but extended a hand, and John shook it, his grip firm. Something from Will that had stuck around.

Ebner retreated from John's shop. He put a palm to the paper bag sitting in the front seat, all the frozen things inside. He felt the vanilla ice cream. It was still cold.

Ebner sighed again, looking at the shop. He could hear John clanging inside, reshaping the fence. Was John right? Was the only way for Fleet to survive was outside money and Ebner was too stubborn to see it?

And would it be the same if Fuchs got his hands on it? And did that even matter?

You're damn right it matters, Ebner. This is our place. Don't forget it.

The echo of Will's voice rang sharply, and the coldness in Ebner's heart warmed for a moment. John hadn't committed to anything yet. He could still talk him out of it. Maybe he could talk to Joanna, see what she thought of this whole mess. Maybe she could get through to John. And Morris was right. He should talk to her, anyway. See how she's holding up.

All that could wait, though. He needed to talk to someone else first.

Fuchs. He would get it from the horse's mouth. See what he wanted with Fleet. See if Morris was right about his eyes. Rumor was he had a house out at Sunny Meadows. The first home built. Maybe he'd pay him a visit. All neighborly like.

Ebner grabbed his keys and started his truck. The clutch caught a bit, but it worked fine. He'd have to look at it sometime this week. He drove down the main drag, passing the Dairy Queen, the unofficial marker for the end of Fleet proper. Then a few minutes of trailer parks and neighborhoods filled with small, ranch-style homes. Few people were out working in their yard. Some kids on bikes. There were still folks here. It wasn't a ghost town, not a graveyard. It was a living place, occupied by living people.

The sight of them reassured Ebner. It wasn't just in his head. Fleet wasn't empty, wasn't dead. Not yet.

But then they were past him, and he saw the edge of his property. He had bought it long ago, back when land was cheap and Fleet was still growing. The plant had just opened, and half the town worked there, including him and Will. No one wanted the land. It had been a cattle washing station, and all the crap they treated the cows with had washed off into the soil. It would have taken a fortune to get it cleaned up. So the previous owner had sold it to him, and Ebner had plans for it.

Never happened, though. He'd done just enough to keep it hospitable, but only just enough. Never turned it into something. Who knows, maybe Fuchs didn't want his land. Maybe he only had ideas for the main drag. Some local investment opportunities.

Ebner turned down his long driveway. He'd never had a gate, never saw the need for one.

He spotted the car well before he got to the end of the driveway. A white BMW, as far as he could tell. New. Clean. It shined under the early afternoon sun.

Who the hell?

But he should have known. He pulled up and a man stood on the porch, smiling and waving, a grin as wide as the ocean. Ebner hadn't even seen him before, hadn't been introduced, but he knew who it was.

It was Fuchs, plain as day.

'Cause Morris was right.

Ebner knew it was Fuchs, just by looking at him. He could see it in his eyes.

3

Ebner forgot his groceries. He flipped off the ignition and stepped down from the pickup truck.

"What are you doing on my property?" he asked, even if he already knew the answer. Fuchs didn't leave his porch, waiting for him, extending a hand. Ebner got a good look at him.

Morris was right. He was tall. Taller than Ebner by a couple of inches, his blond hair cut short, and swept back, kept down with some kind of product. He was handsome, with high cheekbones and a thin nose, a sharp jawline.

He had broad shoulders and a tight waist, dressed in a subtle gray suit that fit him perfectly. Ebner didn't know fashion that well, but he could tell that suit was worth more than Ebner's truck, most likely. Fuchs was the kind of man

Ebner would have gone after in his younger days, maybe, but even Ebner in his younger days would have been stopped by his eyes. 'Cause Morris was right about those too.

He understood the comparison to Harper. Who else would Morris be able to compare to, at least anyone Morris had met in his life? Morris had his stint in 'Nam and then spent most of his life afterward here. And nobody who'd come through Fleet had eyes like that. There would always be some crooks and scoundrels who came through, some bad men with evil intent, but nothing like Harper, who had lost the last vestiges of his humanity out in a jungle, out on a mission to kill.

But Ebner didn't see Harper in Fuchs' eyes. At least not mostly. Harper's eyes were terrifying, sure, full of insane confidence. Full of death. Seeing them that day in the rain was all it took to know he was beyond redemption.

Fuchs' eyes were ice blue, striking, but not full of anything.

They were empty.

Devoid of any feeling, or empathy, or humanity. Whatever was behind those eyes, Ebner immediately recognized as something beyond his reckoning. And it scared him.

"Hello, Mr. Graves," said Fuchs, his hand still out. Ebner didn't reach for it. He had thought to shake the man's hand, even if just to get a better handle on him, but he couldn't make himself touch him. Fuchs held his hand out a moment longer, but then pulled it back in, realizing that Ebner wouldn't shake. "I'm Oskar Fuchs. I wanted to introduce myself, and perhaps speak to you for a moment."

Ebner looked up at him a second longer, from the base of his porch, Fuchs not moving from in front of Ebner's small cracker-style wooden house. The longer Ebner looked into his eyes, the smaller he felt. Felt like he'd get so small that Fuchs would swallow him whole, right through his eyes. That Fuchs' eyes weren't empty at all, but contained the entirety of anybody who he'd crossed paths with, anyone who'd met his gaze.

BANG

A car back-fired from the property across the way from Ebner, and it broke him from Fuchs' gaze. He looked to the source, but it only happened once. He was thankful for it.

Ebner couldn't explain it, but he had felt lost in Fuchs' eyes. His heart sped up, back to what Ebner considered normal. He forced a breath in and out.

He avoided looking into his eyes again, walking up the stairs of his porch, onto the same level as Fuchs, past him, standing between him and his door. He already felt better, with his own home at his back.

"I've heard of you," said Ebner. "Around town."

"I hope it was good," said Fuchs, smiling wide again. Ebner was closer now, and the skin on his face was unlined, perfect. It seemed to glisten slightly in the sun. As Ebner backed close to his door, Fuchs ducked into the shade. Ebner didn't answer. His earlier determination to speak to Fuchs had disappeared. Sharing the same space as him made him feel uncomfortable. He wanted Fuchs gone, even if he had answers he wanted.

"May I come inside?" asked Fuchs, eyeing the door.

"We can discuss business out here," said Ebner.

"The heat—"

"If you want to talk to me, you can do it right here," said Ebner. "Otherwise, you can leave."

Fuchs softly exhaled, trying to remain smiling. "Okay then. Well. I'll get straight to business, then. I would like to buy your house and land. All of it."

"I've heard you been making offers all over town," said Ebner. He still wouldn't look in Fuchs' eyes. "That true?"

"I've made some offers, yes," said Fuchs. "I see an opportunity in Fleet."

"What would that be?" asked Ebner.

"A chance for growth," said Fuchs. "Sunny Meadows will soon be full of new residents, and those residents will need places to eat, to shop, to play. Fleet is the closest city by far, and with the right amount of capital, it will blossom into a lovely place."

"Doesn't seem like Sunny Meadows has enough people to keep all that stuff afloat," said Ebner.

"Sunny Meadows is just the start, Mr. Graves," said Fuchs. "That's why I want to talk to you. Why I want to purchase your land. It is a puzzle piece I require, that will fill in the next step of my plan."

"That so?"

"Yes," said Fuchs. "I consider myself an honest man, Mr. Graves. Your land will become another development, connecting Sunny Meadows to Fleet proper. The roads will connect and share the same infrastructure. I have done this in multiple places throughout the country, and it has proved most successful every time."

As Fuchs spoke, Ebner listened to his voice. It had a certain rhythmic quality to it, comforting but stern all at once. He had an accent but Ebner couldn't place it. It was nothing he'd ever heard before.

"Where are you from, Mr. Fuchs?" asked Ebner.

"What?" asked Fuchs.

"Where are you from? Where is your home?" asked Ebner.

"Ah, yes. Europe," said Fuchs. "Poland."

"I don't think I've ever heard your accent before," said Ebner.

"Well, I've traveled much throughout my life, and so my accent tends to wander as well," said Fuchs, smiling still. "About my offer."

"What about it?" asked Ebner.

"Well, I assume you would like to hear it," said Fuchs.

"You know what they say about assuming things," said Ebner.

Fuchs' face showed confusion for the first time. "I—I don't follow."

"It makes an ass out of you and me," said Ebner.

Fuchs laughed, an alien sound erupting from his throat. Ebner gritted his teeth. "I like that, Mr. Graves. I would like to get out of this heat, so I will make my offer. Five million, for everything, in a single payment, deposited wherever you would like."

Ebner had expected a large offer, more than the land was rightful worth, but he hadn't expected seven figures. And he had planned on saying no, no matter how much the offer was. On principle alone. But principle is well and good until it meets the real world, where issues of black and white turn gray.

His heart jumped into his throat at the thought of so much money, more than he had earned in his entire life. But still, what would it get him?

A bigger house. A new truck. Travel, if he wanted.

But it wouldn't make Fleet what it once was.

And it wouldn't bring William back.

It all flew through his head in an instant, his face as still and staid as ever. Fuchs watched him, he knew, waiting, reading him. He knew the number was big because he guessed it was nothing to Fuchs. A substantial offer to a hick out in the boonies, who'd say yes, sell him his land, and get out of his way.

"No," said Ebner.

"No?" asked Fuchs. Ebner heard doubt in his voice for the first time, and he mustered up the guts to look him in the eyes again, ready to break contact if necessary. Their eyes met, and whatever power they once had, it was gone now. The confidence Fuchs projected earlier wavered. "You heard me correctly?"

"Yeah, five million. Five, followed by six zeroes. Don't matter. I'm not selling."

"Mr. Graves, it is an incredibly generous offer—"

"What are you planning to do with Fleet, Mr. Fuchs?" asked Ebner.

"I told you," said Fuchs. "I'm investing in its growth. I'm going to bring in new stores, new restaurants."

"I'm not talking about the land," said Ebner.

"I don't follow," said Fuchs.

"The people," said Ebner. "What about the people in town? What are your plans for them?"

"Well, my investments will also create work. We will need managers, cooks, staff. Hundreds of jobs."

"So you'll buy up their stores, and their mom and pop restaurants that they already worked at, and then hire them back for less pay and at some place they don't have any ownership of?"

"I don't think—"

"I know your game," said Ebner. "And you're not buying this town out from under us."

"The vast majority have already agreed to sell," said Fuchs. "The contracts are getting finalized right now."

"That's nice," said Ebner. "I'm still not selling."

"Ten million," said Fuchs. "I'll double it."

"What am I going to do with ten million that I can't do with five?" asked Ebner.

Ebner saw the frustration bubble up to the surface of Fuchs for the first time, his eyes narrowing just for a moment, anger cracking his facade.

"Fine," said Fuchs. "I'll give you an ownership stake in everything. 5%. Over time, you will make far more, and have a say in how we develop. And a home in the new development. It could even be in this very spot."

"No."

Fuchs balled his hands into fists, once, twice, and Ebner saw something else in his face, something change, for just a moment, and then it vanished. That's when he noticed the sweat beading on Fuchs' forehead, but it wasn't just perspiration. It was white bleeding off of him.

What in the hell?

"You are a frustrating man, Mr. Graves," said Fuchs.

"I can be."

"I'm trying to save this city," said Fuchs. "Without my help, Fleet will be dead within ten years. And you might as well. Why not try and save it? Why not try and use what little time you have left, and spend it enjoying yourself?"

"Some things are better off dead, Mr. Fuchs. I'm not interested in selling. Get off my property. If you come back, I'm calling the police."

Fuchs stared at him a moment longer, and Ebner felt that pull, all of a sudden, but it wavered and then disappeared, and Fuchs turned quickly, marching back to the car, shielding his eyes from the sun with a hand.

The BMW started and then took off down the driveway. Ebner watched him go. He allowed himself a smirk.

Then he realized what the white liquid was dripping down Fuchs' forehead.

It was sunscreen.

And then he remembered the groceries.

"Oh, goddamnit!" he yelled, jogging as fast as his old bones would allow. He went to the bag in the cab of the truck, but he could already see the sodden paper on the bottom. It was what remained of the ice cream.

"Fuck."

4

"Is this life enough for you?"

They laid in bed, the night deep and dark above them. Ebner knew it was past 3, maybe even past 4, but he didn't want to go to sleep. He didn't want to admit the night was over, that it was time for William to drive back home. He never did, not ever, the one or two nights a month where Will would come over for dinner, for a "boy's night". That's what Will told Joanna.

"What do you mean?" asked Ebner. They were young still, then. John wouldn't be born for three years.

"This," said Will. Will's gentle voice lilted in the dark. "I don't know if we'll ever be more than this."

Ebner laid silent in the darkness. Clouds covered the moon that night, and he felt Will's warmth against him.

Ebner had thought about it, of course he had, long shifts at the plant, his mind wandering to what his life would be. But he hadn't done anything about it. Never said nothing to Will. They had this much, and he didn't want to lose it.

"It might be," said Ebner, finally. That's the one thing Will always did, always knew. Always knew if he was quiet long enough, Ebner would answer.

"I'm asking Joanna to marry me," said Will.

The words hung there, heavy, slowly sinking.

A surge of coldness hit Ebner in his heart, but he said nothing, didn't move. The pain was familiar, expected. The pain had been there when Will dated her for the first time, when they became an item. William loved her, no doubt about it, and she loved him. Ebner saw it in their eyes. So he didn't make Will choose. Didn't set out no ultimatum.

The reality was right outside, every day. Ebner and Will could never be public, not in this life. And so Ebner took that pain, and endured it, for these nights, where Will's body warmed his lean frame and his calluses softly grazed his chest.

Ebner said nothing, for a long time, only took Will and hugged him close, burying his face into the back of Will's neck, his stubble rasping across his skin. Will let him have his silence.

"It's enough for now," said Ebner. "If it ever ain't, I'll tell you. Alright?"

"Alright," said Will.

They laid there in the dark.

"I'll still love you," said Will. "Won't change that."

"I know it," said Ebner.

"I have to go," said Will. "Sun's rising soon. Need to get

back."

"Another five minutes," said Ebner. "Just five more."

Will turned, and kissed him, soft at first, and then harder. "It's never five more minutes—"

Ebner reached for him and then he was awake, alone, the bed empty, as it ever would be.

He looked at his clock, solid red numbers in the dark, and it was an hour until he normally woke up, no alarm set, no need anymore. But he didn't go back to sleep, didn't bother. He never could after those dreams.

He got up, drank his coffee, and read his paper. Thought about what he wanted to get done today.

It had been a few days since his discussion with Fuchs. The prospect of him still lingered there, somewhere in Ebner's mind, but it was tenuous still. Without Ebner's land, Fuchs couldn't fulfill his plan the way he wanted. Would that change anything?

Thoughts like those filtered down through Ebner's mind, but he still had his daily life to attend to. He couldn't sit around all day waiting for Fuchs to cause more trouble.

The discussion with Fuchs had brought up something else though in his mind, about Ebner's oh so coveted plot of land, and how much of it had fallen into disrepair. He had planned today to go have a look at it. Take a nice walk through the brush and woods and see what he could do about some of it. Scope it out.

As the sun rose, Ebner emptied his coffee mug and put together his gear. Boots, gloves, machete to cut through the heavy brush. Probably should bring a big jug of water, because it'd still be hot as hades in the middle of the day. Get himself his big hat. Sunscreen. He could still hear Will's voice inside his head, telling him to wear his damn sunscreen.

But every time he went to grab something, or to hunt down the tube of sunscreen, he would wander. He'd lose focus, his mind spinning back around to that dream. To William, to the life they had, and to John, and then to his near argument with John the other day, and then to Fuchs, and it all spun back around.

By the time he'd finally found the damn gloves—they were tucked behind his big hat—he knew he wouldn't be able to get any work done today. Instead, he changed into a collared shirt and a clean pair of blue jeans, and hopped into his truck.

Edna's Floral was empty when he stepped in, not too odd for a random weekday, he supposed. And flowers weren't invincible against Fleet's downturn anyways. Edna gave him the usual. Ebner only ever came in for one reason anyway.

Then back in the truck, for what would replace his trip through his property.

Fleet Cemetery was outside of the city limits, west, on the other end of town from his house and Sunny Meadows. It was a pleasant drive, with the driver side window rolled down, the wind rustling the blue roses propped up in the passenger seat. All the confusion and lack of focus from earlier in the morning was gone, which told Ebner he'd made the right decision.

He'd expected to find the cemetery empty on a weekend morning. It was just big enough that you couldn't see the back of it standing at the front, but it wasn't much bigger than that.

But it wasn't empty, with a short line of cars out front.

Ebner parked away from them, giving room for their grief, and avoided the ceremony that took place in the front left corner of the graveyard. He eyed it and recognized a few clustered around the grave. Pastor Tompkins gave the eulogy.

Ebner didn't linger though, walking through all the way to the back, the bouquet of blue roses tucked close to his body. He laid them down at the foot of Will's tombstone before wiping away a few stray pieces of dirt from the sides and bottom.

He stood there silently for a moment, and Will let him have his silence.

"I had the dream again," said Ebner, finally. "I know, I know. I can't control my head when I'm sleeping. And it's known you for fifty years. It won't let go easy. I know. But it's still hard, seeing you alive and well and then I wake up and there's nothing there but an empty bed, and there ain't a soul I can talk to about it except for Morris, and even then I can't. He said I could, as much as I want, but I can't pile it onto him. I can't—"

—let go is what you were going to say, but you can't even tell Will.

Ebner exhaled, and breathed in deep, before tears formed.

"I don't know what to do about John," said Ebner. "I've talked to him, and he says he hasn't made up his mind to sell the shop or not, but I saw the look in his eyes. I don't like it. Fuchs is young and rich and full of promises. I can't compete with that."

The wind blew by, hard, and Ebner could briefly hear the pastor speak, his loud, deep voice carrying. The breeze slowed, and it disappeared.

"I've really tried to be a voice of reason in all this, but I don't know what else to do. I don't want him to lose the shop, to lose ownership of this place." Ebner took another breath. "Especially to a man like Fuchs. Something's not right about him. I don't know what it is, but I don't like him. You wouldn't either. He's hiding something."

Ebner kneeled, his hips, knees, and back creaking, but he did it anyway. "I don't think John knows what to do anymore. I guess I don't blame him. I don't rightly know either. You were holding everything together, Will. Without you—"

Without you, I don't see much reason to keep keeping on.

Ebner touched the earth, warm from the morning sun. "I'll try, though. I know it'd be the easiest thing in the world to sell to Fuchs, and let John go, take Jo with him and move to someplace better. But everything I ever wanted was here. I don't want to see it different. I don't want to see someplace else. I want—"

But Ebner couldn't finish that sentence. He'd run out of words for Will. But he didn't leave, not then. He knelt there, his hand on the warm earth, knelt until his ankles cramped and he forced himself up, dizzy from the blood rushing to his head.

"I'll keep trying. I promise. I love you." He turned, and didn't look back, walking to his truck. The funeral had ended, the gravedigger piling dirt on top of the coffin. No one stayed to watch. Most of the cars had gone by then, off to the wake. A few stayed behind, including one Ebner knew, Peter Philip, another longtime Fleet resident, now retired. He stood talking to a younger man who Ebner didn't recognize.

Ebner walked up to them.

"—I don't know what to do myself," said Peter, Ebner catching the end of his sentence. Peter turned to Ebner, extending a hand. Peter was average height, wisps of white hair swirling on his head. He wore a slightly too large suit. Ebner took his hand and shook it. "Ebner."

"Peter," said Ebner.

"This is Tom," said Peter. "Tom Parkins. Owns the tractor dealership out on Route 19."

"Nice to meet you," said Ebner, and Tom returned it with a handshake. "My condolences."

"Appreciate it," said Peter.

"Can I ask—who was it?" asked Ebner.

"You hadn't heard?" asked Peter.

"I guess not," said Ebner.

"Al," said Peter.

"Al Snyder?" asked Ebner. "Holy shit. I thought he'd live forever. Made out of stone. Sorry, Pete. I knew you two were close."

"S'alright," said Peter. "He was a good one."

"What's going to happen to his land?" asked Ebner.

"Don't know," said Peter. "Got no relatives, far as I know. Never had a will drawn up either."

"Think it goes to the state," said Tom. "And they decide what to do with it. Imagine they'll sell it."

"Guess he wasn't expecting to go," said Ebner.

"Who does?" asked Pete. "Even when things are bad."

"How—how did it happen? If it isn't too much to ask," said Ebner.

"You know me, I ain't squeamish," said Pete. "Al's up in Heaven, cursing at angels, most likely." Pete paused. "Some animal got him. Something terrible. Officer Angle was there, said it was the damndest thing he'd ever seen. Puked his guts out at the sight of it."

"Animals?" asked Ebner. "Like what?"

"Think they said wolves," said Pete. "That or a bear, but we don't get bears here anymore. Must have been driven out of their land, hungry. Al was out in his yard. Might trying to chase them off, and they attacked."

"That don't sound right," said Ebner.

"Who knows?" asked Pete. "Weird shit happens sometimes. Say, Ebner—you get an offer from that Fuchs fella?"

"Yeah," said Ebner. "Yeah, I did."

"What did you tell him?" asked Pete.

"Told him no," said Ebner. "I like having my land and my town more than I like the money."

"That's what I figured," said Pete. "He offered a pretty penny for our little plot of land. Near had a heart attack when I heard the number. But the missus asked what'd we do with all of it, at our age. And she was right. Us old-timers is the only ones saying no, is what I heard."

"Thank Jesus for it," said Tom. "God knows what the town will be."

A thought entered Ebner's mind, something dark, with hooks.

"Pete, did Al get an offer from Fuchs?" asked Ebner.

"Yeah, he did," said Pete. "He's right on the other side of Sunny Meadows. Can't imagine it wasn't generous. Fuchs wants that land. But Al said no, just like us. He didn't know anything else but his farm."

Ebner nodded. "Thanks Pete. Again, condolences." The two shook hands with Ebner before Ebner left, driving back to his house, with still enough time to survey his land.

But his thoughts weren't any clearer than it they'd been when he started. Al's death weighed heavy on his mind. They hadn't been close, but they knew each other, both living in Fleet their whole lives. And Al had the same reaction to Fuchs that Ebner did. A rejection of a big money offer.

And now he was dead.

5

A few days later, the phone rang. Ebner had come in for a drink of water. He answered, Morris' voice on the other end.

"I need your help down here, Ebner," said Morris. He sounded scared. "You should bring that axe handle. Maybe the shotgun."

"What's going on?" asked Ebner.

"There's men down here chasing away my customers," said Morris. "I need your thunder."

"Be there soon," said Ebner, and hung up. He threw on a clean shirt, and grabbed the axe handle from the shed, and tossed it in the cab of his truck. He stared at the shotgun for a long second, but opted it against it. Things would have to be bad for him to take the double barrel into town.

The handle would have to be enough today. He hoped he

wouldn't need to use it.

Ebner arrived at Morris' store seven minutes later. He parked, and immediately saw the three men standing right by the entrance, under the short overhang. He grabbed the handle, old, made from hardwood, the head long forgotten. It had ceased to be an axe a long time ago. It was just a club now.

Ebner walked to the entrance, holding the cudgel in one hand. The three men leaned up against the wall all stood, moving in between him and the door. He didn't recognize two of them, but the third—the third he knew. Someone's grandson. Met him at some function, at somebody's birthday or retirement party. The other two might be local, but he doubted it.

Morris hadn't told him, but Ebner knew before he jumped in his truck that Fuchs had sent these men here. He wanted Morris' property, and he would do whatever was necessary to get it.

One of the two he didn't recognize led them, putting his hand up, not quite touching Ebner, but he would if Ebner kept walking. Ebner would play their game.

"Excuse me," said Ebner. "I need to go inside."

"Oh, I wouldn't go in there, old timer," said the man. He wore a white shirt, their leader. The other unknown wore a blue polo. The familiar kid was dressed in jeans and a black t-shirt. "The owner said some not so nice things about the town and its people. I wouldn't give him your business, if I were you."

"You're not me," said Ebner. "And put your hand down. If you touch me, I'm going to put your dick in the dirt."

"No need to talk like that, old timer," said the man, but

he lowered his hand.

"I would say there is," said Ebner. "I would say that you're lying about a good friend of mine, probably my best friend left. So I'd say my language is appropriate. Fuchs send you?"

"It doesn't matter—"

"Because I was polite the last time we talked," said Ebner, cutting him off. "But next time I won't be. Next time I see him I'm going to smash his fucking teeth down his throat."

"Mr. Fuchs wants what's best for us," said the man Ebner recognized. The leader glanced at him and sighed.

"Shut your mouth, Tim," said the leader.

"I remember now," said Ebner. "Timmy. Little Timmy Conner. Chuck and Ashley's boy. Your folks know you're doing this?"

He only stared back, his face growing red.

"Or your grandmother?" asked Ebner. "How she doing by the way? How she feel having a deceitful bully as a grandson?"

He didn't answer, but Ebner saw the fear in his eyes. He remembered Ebner, now. The other two didn't know him.

"Old man, you shut your mouth and listen. Mr. Fuchs has a plan for our community, and you're standing in the—"

"Our community?" asked Ebner. "When you move to Sunny Meadow? A month or two ago? Strange how fast you think you own something." Ebner squeezed the handle in his hand, his grip firm. "I'm going inside my friend's store." He walked, right toward the three of them.

"You wait—" said the leader, putting his hand up again, and his fingers grazed Ebner's chest, and that was enough.

Ebner tapped the handle once on the ground and then swung it hard, using his long arms as leverage, whipping it quickly into the leader's side as hard as he could. Once upon a time, Ebner never would have swung it with all his force. He knew how much damage the club could do, especially with all his strength behind it.

But that's when he was a younger man, 185 pounds of lean, solid muscle from hammering on metal all day. He was an old man now, an old timer, as this kid had said, and he couldn't afford to hold back. He had to swing as hard as he could, and hope it was enough.

Today, it was enough. The leader in the white shirt took the club right in the side, and Ebner heard a rib crack. Maybe two. The kid grunted, a short hard sound of pain and surprise. He fell, holding his side, the air driven out of him. Blue polo came at him then and Ebner grabbed the handle with two hands and swung it into his stomach with a deep, awful thud. He fell too, holding his gut.

"How about you, Timmy?" asked Ebner. Tim looked at him, his eyes full of fear. He turned and ran. Ebner peered down at the two others, still rolling on the ground. "Don't be here when I come back out."

Ebner went inside. Morris stood behind the register, peering out, trying to see what had happened.

"Oh, thank God it's you," said Morris. "Did you bring the shotgun?"

"No, just this," said Ebner. "It was enough. Two of them are down, and Timmy went a-running."

"You think they'll call the police?" asked Morris.

"Maybe," said Ebner. "Does Fuchs have the Sheriff in his pocket yet?"

"I doubt it," said Morris. "Hicks is a hard ass who hates rich folk. But I don't know. Fuchs might get him still."

"I don't think they want the attention," said Ebner. "Not yet, anyway. What did they want?"

"They asked me to reconsider Fuchs' offer. Told me it would be in my best interest to sell," said Morris. "And when I still told them no, and advised them to get off my property, they posted up outside, and scared away customers. I waited for them to get bored, but they weren't."

"So you called in the cavalry," said Ebner.

"I could have called the cops, but I doubt they would have done anything," said Morris. "Least nothing useful."

"This won't be the end," said Ebner. "You hear about Al Snyder?"

"Yeah, it's a shame," said Morris. "I liked Al."

"You don't think anything about how he died?" asked Ebner.

"They said it was wolves, didn't they?" asked Morris.

"Yeah," said Ebner. "But what wolves would come this close to town? And attack a man on his own property?"

"Don't know," said Morris. "Animals do crazy things sometimes."

"And you don't think it's a coincidence that ole Al didn't want to sell neither? And now his land is going to the state, who'll prolly sell it off?"

"What, you think—you think Fuchs is behind it?" asked Morris. "You think he'd kill somebody?"

"He's trying to intimidate you, isn't he?" asked Ebner.

"Yeah, but sending those three idiots out here is a big difference from killing a man. And it's not like he was shot. He was torn apart. I heard teeth and claws. No man did that. Fuchs would bankrupt me before he would kill me."

"Well, maybe he's trained some animals to do the work

for him," said Ebner.

"Do you really believe that?" asked Morris.

"No," said Ebner. "But something is wrong. It's not a co-incidence. I can't stop thinking about it."

"There ain't much else going on, to be fair," said Morris. "You talked to John lately?"

"Last Sunday," said Ebner.

"You should talk to him again," said Morris. "I saw Fuchs parked at the shop again. They've been talking more."

"He's getting his hooks in him," said Ebner. "I don't know what to do. The harder I push, the harder those hooks set in."

"Eventually, he'll have to make his own decisions," said Morris. "He's a grown man. It's his shop, now."

"They're trying to shut down your store and now you're defending them?"

"I'm not defending anyone," said Morris. "But my reasons for keeping my store have nothing to do with Fleet, Ebner. Look around. This place is going. It may take a long, long time, but I doubt Fleet will be a real town in twenty-five years. You could have called it after the plant closed."

Ebner leaned on the counter, his head down.

"I know it's hard to hear," said Morris. "But John would be better off selling. He's not going to be able to build a life here. And Fuchs is giving him that."

"That's what he's saying," said Ebner. "But Fuchs is bringing in all his money, and a whole bunch of outsiders. And Fleet won't be Fleet anymore."

"So?" asked Morris.

"So it's where I grew up, Morris. You too. And William, and everyone else we know. We built this place, with our blood, and our sweat. Went off to war to fight for it. And then Sunny Meadows got approved without our say-so—"

"Outside the city limits," said Morris. "It's a county matter."

"Either way, it was approved and built within a year, and now it's full of people, and Fuchs wants to shape everything around it to his whims. And swaying anyone in the way with money. And maybe worse."

"What do you want me to tell you, Ebner?" asked Morris. "I tried to talk to him, but John didn't listen to me. He never has. You and his mother are the only ones who's ever gotten through to him. Only reasons he's still here at all."

"I'm going to walk down Main Street, and I won't recognize any of the businesses," said Ebner. "It'll be like walking on Mars."

"You've got to let go of it," said Morris. "Because regardless of what you do, I don't think there's any stopping Fuchs. At least not mostly. He's got too much money."

"I'm not selling to him," said Ebner. "I don't care what he does."

"I'm with you," said Morris. "But he'll probably get it after I'm dead."

"Leave it to me," said Ebner.

"I plan to," said Morris. "I ain't leaving it to my brother. That dumb ass."

"I wasn't being serious," said Ebner.

"I am," said Morris. "After Al, I'm getting a will drawn up. You should do the same."

"It's not a bad idea," said Ebner.

"Thank you for coming down here," said Morris. "You're all I got."

"You need me, you call," said Ebner. "And I mean anything. I don't trust Fuchs, and this won't be the end of it. I'm going to see John, see how he's doing. Try and talk some sense into him."

"Good luck," said Morris. Ebner leaned back up straight, his back already sore from swinging the axe handle. He grabbed it, ready to use it again if the three idiots were waiting for him outside. Morris's voice stopped him before he reached the door.

"Ebner, Al died out in his yard, right?" asked Morris. Ebner turned back.

"Yep," said Ebner. "Cops said he musta been chasing off the animals, and they turned on him."

Morris nodded, his eyes down. He looked up into Ebner's eyes. One of a few who could keep that gaze with him.

"You take care of yourself, too," said Morris. "And maybe don't go outside at night."

"Why you say that?" asked Ebner.

"I've been hearing things, in the dark," said Morris. "It's probably nothing. Wind playing tricks on me. But after Al—I think I'll be staying inside. Be safe."

"You too," said Ebner, and left. The two men he'd beat were gone now. He'd put the fear of God into them.

He hoped it was the end of it. Because if it was more than that, he might need the shotgun.

6

Ebner's gut ached as he pulled up to John's shop. He didn't want to talk to John. He wanted John to see the truth, to see how Fuchs was manipulating him. But his gut ached because he didn't think John could see it, and his gut ached because he was going to try anyway, and probably fail.

John was working on the fences when Ebner entered, pushing the pain in his stomach as far away as he could. The small stack of fencing had grown, now piles and piles of metal. John was smoothing off edges and applying finishing touches with decorative corners and tops.

"Those are looking good," said Ebner. John looked up from his work and then continued, slowly popping a fancy corner into place. Only when he finished did he look up again.

"Thank you," he said. "Order's almost ready."

"How are you doing, John?" asked Ebner. He didn't want to get into an argument. He knew if it got to that, he had already lost.

"Doing alright," said John. "Order's almost done. Should get the creditors off my back. Mr. Fuchs already has another order coming in, so I can start planning on that after I'm done with this. How're you?"

"Could be better," said Ebner. "Had a rough morning."

"Sorry to hear that," said John. "What's the trouble?"

"Just came from Morris' store. Had to run off a few fellas that were causing him trouble. Trying to scare away customers."

"Why would anyone do a thing like that?" asked John.

"They were Fuchs' men, John." Ebner looked at him, trying to keep his emotion away. Stick to the facts.

"Do you know that for sure?" asked John.

"They told me it themselves," said Ebner. "So yeah, I'm pretty sure."

"I'm sure they had their reasons," said John.

"Yeah, they had their reasons," said Ebner. "They want to force Morris out of business, so he has to sell, and Fuchs can get a stranglehold on the town."

"They might have done that all on their own," said John. "No telling if Mr. Fuchs told them to go down and do it."

"You really believe that?" asked Ebner.

"It's inside the realm of possibility," said John.

"When a man shows you what he is, believe him," said Ebner. "Fuchs may say that he has the best interests of the town in mind, but he just wants to own it all. He's a businessman, John. Money is all he cares about. He doesn't care about Fleet."

John sighed. "Morris should sell, Ebner. That hardware store hasn't done good business in ten years."

"Twenty," said Ebner. "You defending him, now?"

"He's trying to help us, Ebner," said John. "And he's doing his best to make people see the right path. You can't talk Morris out of anything once he's got his mind set on it."

"So, you're telling me, the right path is making a man sell his hardware store, the only thing he's ever had? Making him give up his legacy before he's even passed on?"

"It's not like he's stealing it from him," said John. "He's paying top dollar for it. Morris could retire anywhere he wants with it."

"All he wants is to run his store until he dies," said Ebner. "It ain't complicated. And there isn't no amount of money that will give him that."

John looked at Ebner for a moment longer, and then went back to work.

"Are you planning on selling, John?" asked Ebner.

John stopped again. Looked at Ebner.

"I'm thinking about it," said John.

"You can't sell to him," said Ebner. "We have to stay strong."

"For what?"

"What do you mean, for what?"

"What am I staying strong for, Ebner?" asked John. "What am I defending by not selling my shop? And make no mistake, that's what it is. It is *my* shop. Not yours. Not Fleet's. It is *mine*."

"You grew up here," said Ebner. "This town is as much yours as anyone. Why would you want it to change?"

"Ebner, what do you see, when you drive down Main Street?" asked John.

"I see family-owned businesses, struggling," said Ebner. "I see potential. I see a good place, brought low, but still capable of rising again."

"You see your memory of a place," said John. "That's what you see, Ebner. You see a Main Street from fifty years ago, when the plant was operating at full capacity, and the town was growing, not shrinking. You see a place that does not exist anymore."

"That's not—"

"When I look at Main Street, I see a dying place," said John. "And this isn't new. This has been happening for twenty years. I came out of high school, and seeing with my own two eyes this town shrinking and shrinking. I wanted to go to college, get a degree, but Dad told me the machining plant would teach me what I needed. Told me it was a reliable career, that would keep me close to him and Mom. *You* told me it was a safe job. And what happened?"

Ebner didn't answer, only stared at him.

"The plant closed, Ebner, five years later. And that was it, Ebner. I knew it then, but everyone else around here stuck their head in the sand, and continued on, acted like a nuclear blast hadn't gone off in our own backyard. But it had. There was no more living here. Only surviving. Fighting off attrition, hoping to be the last one standing. Sure, some farmers will be alright, but a few farmers can't sustain a whole town."

"I sold you the shop," said Ebner.

"You did," said John. "At a fair price. But there is even less work now than there was then, and there's no putting that off. I don't want to struggle my entire life. Mr. Fuchs is giving me a way out. He's giving Fleet a way out."

"It won't be Fleet anymore," said Ebner.

"You keep saying that," said John. "But what does it matter if Mr. Fuchs changes the town? What does it matter if it isn't what it was?"

"The people, John," said Ebner. "The people matter."

"What do you think would happen to them if we don't sell?" asked John.

"There are more than two choices," said Ebner. "If Fuchs really wants to help the town, he could try and support these local businesses. Give people loans, or support small shops in the area with all his money."

"Why would he do that?" asked John. "What sense does it make to put these places on life support when what they really need is a funeral?"

"Listen to yourself," said Ebner. "These are *people*. These are the people you grew up around."

"And they'll still be here," said John. "And be able to actually survive. Thrive even. Mr. Fuchs is offering a future, Ebner. What are you offering?"

Ebner felt his chest tense, felt anger rising, an argument coming. He wouldn't be able to talk much longer. Ebner remembered Will's words, of talking to the boy, but talk wouldn't do it anymore. He turned away and took a deep breath. Blinked his eyes hard, once, twice.

"You hear about Al Snyder?" asked Ebner.

"Yeah, I heard," said John. "It's a shame."

"Fuchs had made him an offer for his land," said Ebner. "Al had turned him down."

"Doesn't surprise me," said John. "Al was stubborn, just

like Morris. Like you."

"You don't find it suspicious that Al dies within a week of turning down Fuchs' offer? Especially considering his land goes to the state, who're most likely going to sell it?"

"Al got killed by some animals or something," said John. "Got torn apart. Don't tell me you think Mr. Fuchs did that too?"

"There's a pattern, John," said Ebner. "Direct attacks on anyone who's getting in his way."

"I can't say that the three fellas at Morris' was the right thing to do," said John. "I'll talk to Mr. Fuchs about it. I'm sure it was just a misunderstanding. But now you're accusing him of murder? Of what, siccing wild animals on people? Do you know how crazy that sounds?"

"I'll bet you dollars to donuts that Fuchs ends up owning that land, and tearing down Al's farm, and building up a bunch of houses on it," said Ebner. "Who benefited from Al's death? Fuchs does."

"He was torn apart, Ebner," said John. "Mr. Fuchs is just a businessman. He isn't the Devil, and he doesn't control wild animals."

Ebner breathed hard. His heart rate was up. He wanted to scream, but he forced it down. He looked at John, and he saw Will's eyes peering out, looking right at him, and all that anger was replaced by pain.

"I see him, you know?" said Ebner. "Every time I look at you, I see him."

"I know you do," said John. "Can't help it. And maybe things would be different if he was still here. But he's not. Dad's gone, Ebner. Believe me, it hurts me too. But we have to move on. Fleet is dying, and I don't want to die with it."

7

Ebner pulled up to Will and Joanna's house—*just hers, now, Ebner*—and put his truck into park, sitting with the engine idling and the AC running. He didn't want to burn up in the heat, but he also wanted to give her a good warning that he was here. He hadn't called—he should've called—but he hadn't, and the best he could do was sit there in plain sight for a few minutes, and give her a chance to get ready for his arrival, good or bad.

Ebner had never hated Joanna. Not once. He'd been jealous of her, sure. Disliked her, from time to time. Hated the situation. Even hated Will. A deep, dark hatred that had arisen once or twice in their long relationship that they had mended over time.

Never her, though. It wasn't her fault, and Ebner had

never blamed her for his life. She was a good woman, hard-nosed, and tough as a coffin nail. He saw a lot of him in her, and it made sense. Will had a type, and he went strong for it.

Had she ever hated him?

Ebner didn't know, wouldn't ever know, because Jo wouldn't tell him without the question, and Ebner sure as hell would never ask. She might have, once upon a time. He took up a lot of Will's time and energy. Ebner wasn't privy to their conversations, but Will had always cut time in his life for Ebner. A night or two a month at Ebner's place. One monthly dinner at Will's place with all of them, and another at Ebner's tiny house, even after John was born.

There'd be interruptions, and arguments, and resentment, and jealousy, but they'd kept going. All three, and then four of them.

William stared at Jo's house, and he saw the front curtain part a few inches. He didn't see her face, but it could only be her looking out. She had seen his truck. He'd give her a few more minutes.

Did she know about them? Did she know the truth?

The question had kept Ebner awake at night for a time. Because she held the pin to that grenade, and she could pull it at any time, and destroy all their lives. Especially after John was born. And the way she looked at him sometime— it felt like she was thinking it over in her head. If pulling that pin was worth it.

But maybe Ebner had misread her. Her eyes, like his, were unyielding, and looking at her was the lone time when Ebner knew what other people felt when they stared into his. Maybe she thought only that Ebner and Will's relationship was what they told everyone, or at least led everyone to believe. Best friends, who had worked together for thirty years. True to each other, through thick and thin. Ebner could basically read people's mind after a time, just through their eyes, when they saw the two of them. He heard the whispers without listening.

You don't think, do you? Those two? Those two Texas rednecks? Ain't possible.

I would say so, but Will's married. Got himself a kid and a wife. Sure they spend time together, but Will's about the only man alive who can stand being around Ebner for more than ten minutes.

Sure, you can see something in their eyes, once and a while, but I couldn't believe them two being queer. Hell, Ebner once near killed me just by staring at me.

For a couple years after Brokeback Mountain came out he worried, but nothing came of it either. He never saw the movie. He was afraid it would kill him. Almost watched it, one night. He liked that Heath Ledger. But he didn't know if he could take all that pain.

Most people believed they was just best friends. And maybe Jo thought that too, and maybe Ebner didn't want a partner long-term. Or that he was such a bastard no one would stay with him. But Ebner didn't believe that. Jo was smart.

What was probably true is that she suspected. How much, he didn't know, but he would guess it was some. She might have suspected something about Ebner. How a Texas redneck never once talked about women. How she never caught him glancing at her, especially when she was younger. Jo was an attractive woman, and she knew it. Will's long nights over at Ebner's, without fail.

But the time without Will had brought him clarity, and if there was anything that made her suspicious it was those nights. Not that they had them, regularly. But that Will never slept over. Not one time, in decades, did Will ever fall asleep at Ebner's.

Ebner hated it, hated that he never got to wake up to Will, but Will told him it was dangerous. Told him how it would get people talking, and how one time would turn to two would turn to three. And it was hard for Ebner to disagree.

But never, in all those years, did Will fall asleep at Ebner's. He'd crawl into bed next to Joanna at 4 or 5 AM, but never did he falter.

And when Ebner stopped to think about it, how was that possible? Ebner and Will always told people they just played cards, drank, and bullshit those nights. Which wasn't entirely a lie. But to think, over hundreds and hundreds of nights, for Will to *never* accidentally fall asleep? How was that possible? Everyone was human.

The only way it was possible if Will knew it would raise suspicion, and so he never let it happen. Which was suspicious in its own right.

So he bet Jo suspected something. But it was never enough to pull that pin.

Truth be told, he stopped worrying about it after a few years. Sometimes she'd give him that look, that unyielding glare, but by then Ebner had figured she wasn't debating to blow up that grenade.

What she was doing was making sure he still loved Will, with a love that would match hers. And whatever she saw in him, it was enough. They always had that bond, something no one else in the world had, not even John. That deep dedicated love for Will, so deep it couldn't be severed, not even with hate. Or death.

And just like Jo's true feelings about him, he would never know unless he asked. And he wouldn't, not in this life.

He got out of his truck, walking up the small path of tiled stone that led to her front door. He walked up the steps of their two-story house, now empty except for her, and knocked on the door.

She had known he was there, but she still let him wait on the porch for thirty seconds. Ebner didn't hold it against her. He would have done the same if someone dropped by without warning. The door opened. Jo stood there, her handsome face, long white hair, and hard dark eyes staring back.

"Wasn't expecting you, Ebner," said Jo, standing in the doorway.

"My apologies," said Ebner. He extended a hand, and she took it, softly shaking it. "Thought it was about time for a visit."

"You're not wrong," said Jo. "Come in, I was just doing the dishes."

"Sorry to interrupt," said Ebner. She turned and walked down the hallway toward the kitchen. She hadn't redecorated much since Will had left them. The house looked the same.

"Dishes aren't going anywhere," she said. "Take a seat. Can I get you anything?"

"Some water would be nice," said Ebner. "I could use some."

Jo grabbed a glass and filled it from the tap, and Ebner

took a seat at the kitchen table. They had a dinner table, but it had been used less than a dozen times in the past twenty years. The last time was Will's wake.

She brought it to him and then sat across from him, her wooden chair creaking beneath her. Jo looked at him with unyielding eyes, and he looked right back.

"How you doing, Jo?" asked Ebner, taking a sip of water.

"Alright," said Jo. "Keeping busy. Trying to keep this house from falling apart. You?"

"About the same," said Ebner. "I went and saw Will."

"What'd he tell you?"

"Told me to watch out for John."

"Sounds like him," said Jo. "But John's grown now. Can watch out for himself."

Ebner took another drink, both because he was thirsty and because he wanted to keep his words slow.

"Have you talked to Fuchs yet?" asked Ebner.

"Can't say I have," said Jo. "Heard a lot about him, though."

"From who?"

"From John. A few others, 'round town."

"What do you think?"

"I don't know," said Jo. "Haven't made a judgment, one way or the other."

"I had to drive off some guys from Morris' store," said Ebner. "They work for Fuchs. Trying to pressure Morris to sell."

Jo raised an eyebrow, as if testing his statement for truth, and then lowered it and nodded. It had passed the test.

"Fuchs himself came to my house, wanting to buy my land," said Ebner.

"Must be worth a pretty penny to him," said Jo.

"It is," said Ebner. "But I'm not selling."

"Why not?" asked Jo.

Ebner paused. Another sip of water. "Because it's mine, and not his," said Ebner. "Because I don't want him to control the whole town."

"Ain't much left of Fleet anyways," said Jo.

"Maybe not, but I'd still rather Fuchs not shape it in his image."

"I'm assuming you told John not to sell either?"

"You'd be right," said Ebner. Jo half smiled, her right lip turning up. It wasn't a sign of happiness in her. Ebner'd seen it dozens of times, and it meant that you'd done something Jo disagreed with. "Something wrong?"

"You should let John be the man he wants to be," said Jo.

"He's going to sell the last thing he owns to Fuchs," said Ebner. "It burns me up."

"Might be so, but it's his choice, and not yours," said Jo. "He's old enough. He's not a little kid, not even a young man anymore."

"If you had talked to Fuchs—"

"If I had talked to Fuchs I don't think my mind would change," said Jo. "Least not in letting John decide for himself what he's doing."

"He wants to change Fleet, Jo. He wants it to be a trough for all those pigs living in Sunny Meadows." Ebner felt the steel in his voice, and he tried to call it back, but he couldn't, not about this, and not with Jo, who he knew so well. Jo just stared back at him. That steel would wilt most. Not Jo.

"I don't think you're wrong, Ebner. Fuchs sure has a lot of money, and he's willing to spend it. Make all his problems go away. And that isn't what we're accustomed to. And sure, whatever he makes Fleet into, it won't be what we knew. What we made. It'll probably look and feel empty. Bunch of chain stores. Nothing authentic. Nothing real."

She paused, but she wasn't done, and you didn't interrupt Jo.

"But what does it matter, in the end? Fleet will die without someone stepping in, and doing something. This Fuchs? I don't know him. Probably wouldn't be my friend. But he's made his offer, and John gets to decide to take it or not. Not you, or me, or Morris, or Will, looking down on us. John decides. John decides what kind of man he is, and what his future will be."

Ebner took another drink of water, long this time. He wanted to scream, but he didn't have the words.

"You know that isn't in me," said Ebner.

"I know," said Jo. "You got to let things go sometimes."

"I wish—" Ebner started, but he couldn't find the words.

"Me too," said Jo. "Me too. But John told me if he sells, it's because he wants a future here, a future here in Fleet. And whatever else Fuchs is selling, there's value to that. Because without him, there is no future here. Not for John, and not for the town."

"I was hoping—I was hoping you'd agree with me," said Ebner.

Jo stared at him, with those unyielding eyes. "I want what's best for John, and so do you. That hasn't changed." Another pause. "Will tell you anything else when you visited?"

"He told me to keep trying," said Ebner, his voice catching in his chest. "Don't give up."

"He always did know what to say, didn't he?" asked Jo, her eyes shining.

"He did."

8

The days passed uneasily. Fuchs hadn't contacted him again, and it was radio silent from the rest of his small circle. He wanted to go down and talk to John again, but he knew the more he did, the less it would work.

Ebner kept himself busy with the many chores around the house, with his old westerns, and with tinkering with his truck. He had kept it running this long. He'd make sure that he'd die before it would.

But as the days passed, the tension inside him didn't go away. He hoped that if he put his head down and worked, that everything would work out. That he'd be able to let go of whatever happened to Fleet, to John. To make peace with it. Even with Fuchs. Maybe he'd be able to let it go, like Jo had said.

But that tension didn't go away. It just kept building, up and up, a companion to every chore he did. As he cooked himself dinner, as he worked on the truck, as he hiked through his land, that growing unease served as a constant partner, and no matter how hard he tried to push it away, it stayed put. More than that, it grew. Ate its way through him until it laid right beneath the surface of his skin.

Something was wrong, and he didn't know what. And it was more than Fuchs, and more than John, and more than what would happen to Fleet. Al's death hung in his mind.

It wasn't the first time Ebner had felt like this. After Will's diagnosis, it was the same. He'd cried, alone in his house, after Will told him. But it hadn't made the ache deep inside him go away, and so he'd dug himself into a pit of work to lose himself in. And that normally worked for whatever anxiety he'd had, but it hadn't for that. He had worked himself to the bone, his old body sore for days after, but it hadn't made a difference.

That intense emptiness remained, stalwart and invulnerable inside him, and he hated it, wanted to cut it out, but it stayed put. And this wasn't the same pain, but it was still invincible, unignorable.

He worked on his truck, and the tension seized inside him. He needed to talk to someone. Needed to tell someone. But what he really meant was Morris, because there was nobody else. Morris was his last remaining confidant. He called the hardware store, and the phone rang and rang, with no answer.

It wasn't like Morris. Maybe he was with a customer. Ebner tried again and again, but no answer. He pictured those three men there again, escalating, keeping Morris away from the phone, away from his own business, even trashing the place. And Ebner wouldn't allow that. Maybe that was the source of the poisonous stress inside him. He had known they would take it further, deep down inside, and this was his chance to put an end to it.

The phone kept ringing, so Ebner threw the axe handle back into the truck and drove down to the store, expecting trouble.

But he didn't find it.

The store was closed. It was past noon, and Morris should have been open for hours. He was known to sometimes open the store late, to take a couple hours to sleep off a good drunk. He peeked inside, but everything looked normal.

Where the hell are you, Morris? Home?

Maybe he's sick as hell. Ebner couldn't put it outside the range of possibility, but the tension in his gut, that he was so happy to dissipate, was still there, and it only grew worse as Ebner got back in his truck and headed toward Morris' house, that he had once shared with his late wife. It wasn't that far, inside the city limits, in a small neighborhood next to the lone Fleet office park.

Ebner knew something was wrong as soon as he got out of his truck.

Morris' little car was parked where it always was, but the screen door tipped him off. It clapped in the breeze, slamming every time. *BOP BOP BOP.*

Morris kept the inside door open all the time, to let the breeze blow through, least when he was home. Even sometimes when he wasn't. Didn't worry about burglaries around here, not until lately. But he always latched the screen. Always. Ebner left it unlatched just one time, and Morris wouldn't let him hear the end of it. Not for days, or weeks, or months, but years. Years of "*Latch the screen on your way in, Ebner. Don't forget.*"

But now it flapped open and shut in the breeze, and Ebner reached into the truck and grabbed the club. Something was wrong, and he knew it was right here, right inside, that terrible pain in his guts worse still, now just as bad as when Will told him he was dying.

He walked up the short, crooked front steps of Morris' house and went inside, holding the handle next to him with a tight grip. Ebner didn't latch the screen door behind him, didn't touch anything, because he knew as soon as he stepped inside that this was a crime scene. He could smell the blood, the smell of dark copper. There was a small piece of hope inside him, that somehow he'd find Morris alive, clinging to life, and he could drive him to the ER and he would make it. Hold on for another couple years, that's all he wanted, Morris wanted to make it to 75, a nice respectable number.

The lights were all on, another something wrong, Morris never left the lights on, but then Ebner saw the first sign of blood, much too much blood, pooled, splattered, leading off into the living room, and Ebner looked inside and froze. All that pain and worry coalesced into a single mass and squeezed hard.

What was left of Morris was spread around the room, limbs torn off, decapitated, his guts and entrails draped over the furniture. A string of intestines hung between the two prongs of the rabbit ear antennae. The floor and walls were covered in blood, dried by this point. They had killed him last night, Ebner guessed, but it could have been longer. He guessed it hadn't, because it hadn't rotted yet.

Thoughts flashed through Ebner's mind and then the cruelty and surety of his friend's death seized him, and he had to go outside, his lungs freezing, his breath suddenly impossible to come by. He bent over in Morris' front yard and forced air through his choking throat into his seized lungs. He was going to die out here, be dead, just like Morris, finally see Will again, but then a little air came in, warm and dry, and then they opened up again, and the spots in front of his eyes went away.

Not yet, Ebner. Not yet.

He sat down on Morris' front steps, head in hands. He wanted to collapse, but there was nothing in Ebner that would do it. Something had killed his last, best, friend, and that determination, that cold anger kept the sadness at bay, at least for now. He'd find that sadness later, but right now, all he knew was the same thing that killed Al had killed Morris too.

He took a deep breath, and went back inside, not looking at the bloody floor or the butcher shop that was Morris' living room. He pushed through and picked up the phone, and called the Sheriff's office.

"You didn't touch nothing?" asked Sheriff Hicks. They were at least treating it seriously. Hicks himself had come down to the scene.

"No," said Ebner. "Nothing but the phone to call you. And the screen door, I suppose."

Two other deputies stood outside by their police car. One of them, the younger one, Bobby Green, had puked his guts out after he came out of the house. Ebner didn't blame him.

"When was the last time you saw him?" asked Hicks. Ebner sat on the tailgate of his truck, Hicks taking notes on his little notepad.

"Three days ago," said Ebner. "He had called me to help scare off a few of Fuchs' thugs who were scaring away customers."

"Scaring away customers?" asked Hicks. "We didn't get any reports of that."

"We didn't have no proof," said Ebner. "Woulda been a waste of time. But there was three of them then. All young. Two I didn't know, but the third was Timmy Conner." Hicks wrote more, more scribbling back and forth with his pencil, worn down to the nub.

"Why were they doing that?" asked Hicks.

"Morris wouldn't sell," said Ebner. "Fuchs had made him an offer. Made me one too." More scribbling.

"Anything else happen?" asked Hicks.

"Morris had told me he'd heard noises around the house," said Ebner. "Around the house at night. That he had stopped investigating them. He'd been spooked."

Hicks wrote more down, and then even more.

"Sheriff," said Ebner, and Hicks stopped, looked at him again. "Fuchs is behind this."

Hicks stared at Ebner, but then broke his gaze, looking back at his notepad. "You went in there, right, Ebner?" asked Hicks.

"Yep," said Ebner.

"You think that looks like a man did that?" asked Hicks.

Ebner didn't answer, shifting his jaw back and forth. "It's the same way Al died, Sheriff. Same way. Both of them wouldn't sell to Fuchs, and now they're both dead."

"You didn't answer my question, Ebner. Because you know as well as I do that no man killed Morris. He's spread around the room like a burst pinata. We're still waiting on the CSI guy, but I bet we're going to find claw marks on Morris, just like we did Al. Some animal did this."

"Al lives out on his farm," said Ebner. "So alright, I could buy wolves getting to him, especially out in the open. He feels confident, maybe, thinks he can chase them off, then they surround him. Tear him apart. But where are we, Sheriff? We're in the middle of town. Fleet isn't big, I know, but we're surrounded by houses. The office park is right there, and still gets people coming and going. Even at night, a pack of wolves woulda had to come through town to get here."

"Maybe they're rabid—"

"No wolf is coming through town and attacking someone. And especially not in their own home. What did they do? Knock, and Morris let them in after they asked nicely?"

Hicks sighed. "I know it's hard, Ebner. I know you lost Will, and now Morris, but what other explanation is there? Did Fuchs hire an animal handler? Did he buy a lion from a zoo? Listen to yourself. It don't make no sense."

"All I know is that Fuchs is the only man who benefits from both these men being dead," said Ebner. "You have to do something."

"We're going to sweep the house for evidence, Ebner," said Hicks. "Believe me, once people find out what happened, the whole town is going to go crazy. I'm worried we're going to get bounties on wolves—"

"Were there any tracks at Al's place?" asked Ebner.

Hicks stared at him again. "No," said Hicks. "Nothing."

"There's nothing inside Morris' house, neither. Wolves,

or a bear even, don't clean up after themselves. They can't. There'd be paw prints all over the place. But there's nothing. Tell me how that is." Ebner stared now, hard eyes flashing. Hicks met them for a moment longer, and then looked away, down.

"I don't know, Ebner," said Hicks. "Believe me, I'm trying. But I can't arrest a man just because a couple of deaths were convenient for him. Especially when it looks like they've been torn apart by a monster." As Hicks continued, his voice was lower and lower. "I don't like Fuchs any more than you do, but I can't do anything about it without proof."

"How many people gotta die before you do something?" asked Ebner. "We're at two now. I'm betting there'll be more. More convenient deaths, of people who're getting in his way."

"Listen to yourself, Ebner," said Hicks. "He's a businessman. He's not a killer. None of these people are."

"Then what killed my friend?" asked Ebner loudly. The two deputies looked over.

"I don't know," said Hicks. "I'm doing my best." A van pulled up then. "That's the crime scene guy. I have to go."

"Can I go?" asked Ebner.

"Yes," said Hicks. "Call me if you find any proof." Hicks marched off, shaking the hand of the gentleman who climbed out of the white van. Ebner looked out at the street, sitting on the tailgate. Multiple neighbors stood on their porches, looked through front windows, watching to see what the hubbub was. They'd find out soon enough.

Ebner shut the tailgate with a hard *CLANG* and then climbed into his truck and left, going back home.

The terrible pain inside him never waned. It only grew.

9

"Morris was a good man," said Ebner, looking out over the crowd. "A good man. Not a great one. If Morris was here, he would tell you himself." The crowd chuckled.

Ebner once again stood in Fleet Cemetery, speaking about a man he loved in front of a crowd. The funeral was well attended. Ebner had invited all the old-timers, friends or not. A crowd of well-wishers stood behind the old folks, listening. It was Sunday afternoon, and the late summer sun beat down on them. They all withstood it. They were from Fleet.

"He wasn't great, but he was good. We went to Vietnam together, drafted together. Somehow stuck together through our time over there, and we protected each other. He protected me, and I protected him. In a place where it felt just existing was tempting the grim reaper, we kept each other alive, and made it back here in one piece." Ebner looked over the crowd, into the faces of all the old timers. Most wore sadness, but none of them cried. They all had grown accustomed to death, and its place in their lives. Will, Al, Morris. Three of them dead in less than a year. And none of the assembled thought that'd be the end of it.

"Us protecting each other didn't stop then, though. When we came back home, we still protected each other. Morris was the one who got me the job at the plant, back when it was still running at high capacity. That job changed my life, in ways that neither of us ever predicted. After 'Nam, I was lost, confused about my life. About what to do, like a lot of veterans were. Morris helped give me control again."

Ebner looked, and caught Joanna's eyes, her hard eyes, just like his. She nodded at him once, recognizing him. She always liked Morris, because he'd call her out on her bullshit, just like he did for Ebner.

"It continued, though. As we got older. We protected each other. Once upon a time, over at Rascal's, Morris took a bottle to the head that was meant for me. Luckily, his head is harder than mine. We made that biker regret it. But he protected me. And he never asked for anything in return. Just knowing that he was doing the right thing was good enough for him. He didn't want a reward for being that good man."

Ebner paused, and his eyes passed over the crowd again. He saw John. But then his vision caught who stood next to him.

Fuchs. Ebner felt the anger rise within him.

Don't give him the attention. He wants it. Remember Mor-

ris.

"Morris' store was an extension of him, and he loved it dearly. It was one of the few things in this world that was *his,* and he took care of it. He thought of it as a town institution. Something important. Now, you might say, 'Ebner, it was just a hardware store'. And you might be right. It *was* just a hardware store. But not to Morris. He described it to me as an investment, like the stock market. And I told him, right then, that if he had taken the money he used to build that store and invest it in the stock market, he'd probably have retired a long time ago. It was just a joke, y'know. But it wasn't a joke to him. He was serious, and how he explained it changed how I think about Fleet. And this was probably thirty years ago. He said, 'Ebner, when I say an investment, I don't mean it as a thing that makes me money. I mean it as something that helps my soul. Because I believe having a local place that can sell a man a hammer and some nails as important as going to church. They can build whatever they want with that hammer and nail, and they don't have to drive three towns over to get it from some big store that don't know their name.'"

Ebner looked at Fuchs again, narrowed his eyes briefly, and then looked back over the crowd before he saw Fuchs' reaction.

"So when I say Morris was a good man, I mean it. And when I say he was a good man, and not a great one, I mean that too. Because when I think of a great man, I think of Alexander the Great. The conqueror, back in ancient times. Who grew his empire out to the bounds of the known world. But Alexander wasn't a good man. He was a bad guy. Did bad things. Morris wasn't great. Morris didn't see much outside of Texas. Morris only cared about his store, and his wife, who I pity up there in Heaven, 'cause she's got to deal with him now." The crowd laughed. "But he was a good man, and I'll miss him."

The crowd softly clapped, and then the pastor took over, reciting some verse and a small prayer. When it was time for everyone to bow their head and close their eyes, everyone did.

'Cept Ebner. He kept his eyes wide open, looking right at Fuchs. He studied him, and watched as Fuchs bowed his head, and then stopped, noticing Ebner watching him. And Fuchs stared right back, and Ebner saw his hollow eyes, devoid of sadness, barren. Their eyes locked, and as the pastor prayed, Ebner felt an infinite moment pass, as he tried to find something in Fuchs' gaze.

But he found nothing.

"Amen," said everyone, as the prayer ended, and one by one, they threw dirt on the coffin. An empty coffin, Morris' body in no shape to be assembled ever again.

Ebner resisted his anger, held it at bay while the funeral continued, but as soon as they lowered the coffin, Ebner marched over to Fuchs, who had already started walking back to his BMW, with John at his side. Ebner grabbed him by the shoulder and whipped him around, grabbing at the lapel of his coat with his right hand, balling the fabric in his fist.

Fuchs didn't resist, only eyeing Ebner with a mixture of confusion and disgust.

"What do you think you're doing coming here?" asked Ebner. People already noticed, some waiting and watching, others hurrying back to their car faster.

"What do you mean?" asked Fuchs. John stood next to him, staring at Ebner.

"Ebner, stop this—"

"You shut your mouth, John," said Ebner. "This ain't your business." He turned his attention back to Fuchs. "I mean, how dare you show up to this man's funeral, after everything you've done to this town already."

"I've done nothing to this town," said Fuchs. Up close, Ebner could see the thin sheen of sunscreen covering him. It dripped off of his forehead.

"Don't you fucking lie to my face," said Ebner. "I know what you've done. Maybe you've fooled some of the other people here, but you haven't fooled me. You haven't fooled everyone. And sooner or later, you'll make a mistake, and you'll get caught. And you'll pay."

A slim smile grew on Fuchs' face, a grin that made Ebner uncomfortable. Fuchs had let Ebner hold him, not resisting, but then he reached out with a hand and grabbed the Ebner's own lapel with an incredible strength, and pulled Ebner to him, face to face. Ebner tried to pull away, but it was impossible. Fuchs concealed an impossible power, and he held Ebner there, inches away, and the world disappeared. For both of them, they were the only other thing that existed.

Fuchs studied him, his eyes looking over Ebner's lined face. Fuchs put his head beside him, like they were necking, but then he spoke to him, a just audible whisper that no one but Ebner could hear.

"Morris screamed for mercy as he died," said Fuchs. "He begged for his life as he was ripped apart." And then he dropped Ebner, pushing him to the ground, and Ebner fell hard on his butt, his neck snapping back.

"You son of a bitch," said Ebner, pushing himself back up and charging at Fuchs, but John got in the way, catching him, and then a dozen other arms grabbed him, pulling him back. Fuchs stood there and smiled at him, that slim smile, and then his face was nothing again, and with a look to John, they were gone, walking back to Fuchs' car.

"You're nothing, Fuchs," yelled Ebner, as everyone held him back. "You're nothing but a leech on this town, come to siphon off what little life it has left. You won't get away with it!"

Fuchs didn't turn back, Ebner's words doing nothing.

"Let me go, Goddamnit," said Ebner.

"Calm down, Ebner," said Jo, beside him. "Let him go."

"You didn't hear him," said Ebner.

"You can't do this here, Ebner," said Sheriff Hicks. "Take a breath."

Ebner looked around at the friends and acquaintances holding him back, and Fuchs was driving away, with John in the passenger seat.

Ebner stopped struggling, and everyone let go. He walked to a tree and leaned against it, trying to catch his breath, Fuchs' words echoing in his mind.

He begged for his life as he was ripped apart.

Ebner looked to his suit coat, and saw that it was torn in multiple places when Fuchs had grabbed him. He moved him so easily, without any effort at all.

What was he? And what was going on in Fleet? Ebner's mind raced.

He looked to tell someone, anyone about what Fuchs had told him, but everyone had left him, giving him space.

The anger rose in him again. He would find out who, or what, Fuchs really was. And he'd make him pay for Morris.

10

"Do you think he'll leave?"

They laid together in the dark, much older now. No moon that night.

"I don't know," said Ebner. "I wouldn't blame him if he does."

Will sighed, barely audible, a whisper of a breath. "I don't want him to go," said Will.

"Neither do I," said Ebner. "But what else is there? Without the plant, what's he gonna do?"

"There's still work," said Will.

"Yeah, but no career," said Ebner. "Unless he makes one for himself."

"I'm worried about him," said Will. "About Fleet."

"So am I," said Ebner. He felt Will's breath on his neck,

his callused hand on his chest.

"What about your shop?" asked Will.

"What about it?" asked Ebner.

"Can you hire him on? He can do the work," said Will.

"It isn't about if he can do the work," said Ebner. "There's not enough of it. It keeps me busy, you know that, but I don't make enough to have an employee and pay them a living wage. And that kinda work? Should be making at least twenty bucks an hour."

"What if you found more work?" asked Will.

"I'm half retired," said Ebner. "More than half, honestly."

"I know, Ebner," said Will. Ebner heard the frustration in his voice.

"If you want me to do something, then say it," said Ebner.

A moment of silence from Will. "Sell him the shop. Let him make something of it."

"The shop isn't worth a lot, Will, but it's worth more than what John can pay. He's only been working full time for five years."

Will laid silent, thinking. "Jo and I will loan it to him. We've got plenty."

"You think that will work?" asked Ebner. "You think he can make that an honest living? Enough to raise a family on?"

"I think so," said Will. "Fleet's got enough life left for that."

"And John will want it?" asked Ebner.

"I don't think he wants to leave," said Will. "I want him to stay."

THUNK.

The sound of clanging metal woke Ebner, grasping in

the dark. He blinked awake, his heart beating fast. Was the crash real, or just a memory in his dream?

THUNK.

The noise again, and Ebner knew it was real. Some sound in the dark. Not any noise, his mind doing the invisible work of comparing the catalog of noises he knew of his home and property.

It was the shed door, he was pretty sure. But it didn't happen again. He was awake now, his body complaining from a dozen different joints and muscles, age slowing him down. He forced his way up, sitting on the edge of the bed, rubbing his left knee, warming it up enough to get moving.

He remembered Morris' words. Noises in the dark. Al, going outside to investigate something, and getting torn apart.

This wasn't a coincidence. Ebner was past that now. He was being targeted, the funeral only two days ago, and Fuchs was either taunting him or trying to kill him. Ebner didn't take kindly to either, and considering Morris had been killed indoors, he wasn't safe here either.

His knee was warm enough to move now, still hurting, but functional, and Ebner turned on the bedside light, illuminating his tiny bedroom. He was the only one inside it, and after confirming that, grabbed his shotgun. He had moved it from the high shelf in the closet to next to his bed after the funeral. A double barrel, loaded with buckshot. He reached to the small shelf on his night stand and pulled out a box of ammo, putting a handful of shells in each pocket of his long pajamas. Ebner found his shoes and slipped them on. He looked out his bedroom window, but saw nothing, the light penetrating only a few feet outside.

Clear the house first, Ebner.

His house wasn't big, with only a bedroom, a kitchen, a bathroom, and a living room. A short hallway connected the bedroom and the living room, with the bathroom in between, and he flipped on lights as he went.

The hallway was empty, and he reached into the bathroom to turn on the light, turning in right behind the light, seeing it empty. He turned back to the living room, dimly lit. Ebner cornered the room, seeing nothing but his old furniture and his newer television. He softly stepped to the light switch, and threw it on. Only the kitchen remained. He passed the front door, the deadbolt still engaged. He hadn't heard glass break, so that left only the back door and the kitchen.

The kitchen was dark, the dim light from the living room filtering in, and he flipped on the switch, revealing it to be empty as well. The back door was closed, still locked. Whatever it was, it hadn't been inside.

All the lights inside were on and Ebner looked out the kitchen window, over the sink, which had a clear view of the shed. He could vaguely see it in the dark. The door hung open.

It's a trap, Ebner.

Al had gone out to investigate something. Maybe a loose barn door, flapping in the wind. A strange noise. And that's when they had struck, tearing apart Al in his yard right in front of God.

Ebner knew it was a trap, but he didn't care. They had killed his friend, whatever they were, and he would not let them fuck with him. He didn't know what waited for him out in the dark, but if it could withstand two barrelfuls of buckshot, it didn't matter anyway. It was beyond his reckoning.

Plus, he knew it was a trap. That gave him an advantage, didn't it?

But he wasn't going out there yet. Ebner bet it was waiting on him. Well, it could wait a few minutes longer. Ebner grabbed a heavy flashlight and some duct tape from the utility cabinet and attached the light to the shotgun so he could see and shoot at the same time. He thought to put on a shirt, but he was hot, and he didn't think a layer of cotton was going to stop whatever was out there.

Ebner didn't believe in monsters. Men were bad enough, capable of terrible things. He didn't need to invent something worse to keep his mind occupied. Didn't believe in ghosts neither, or the Loch Ness Monster. He believed what you could see.

So what had killed Al and Morris?

Ebner didn't know. His mind had balanced precariously, thinking a bunch of things at once. Maybe it was trained animals, Fuchs using his money to train a pack of wild dogs to kill on command. Or bears even.

But that didn't explain the lack of tracks. That meant thought and planning. That meant a man. So maybe someone had cleaned up after them.

But nobody had seen anyone coming or going at Morris' place. Which made no damn sense. And made Ebner realize that whatever it had been, whatever it or they were, was something outside of Ebner's imagination, not that it was that wide a boundary. Will had always told him to think outside the box, but Ebner always struggled with it. Working inside the box was easy for him, easy as pie. Outside, not so much.

And so he couldn't imagine what was out there. But he imagined the shotgun would take care of it, if things came to that.

He looked out the kitchen window again, and the shed door still hung loose. The lock that kept it shut was strong. Heavy bolt cutters only thing that could cut it off.

Sweat ran down Ebner's arm, and he wiped it away. He turned on the flashlight and then unlocked the back door, opening it and letting the shotgun lead the way. He swept a full 180 degrees, across his meager backyard, his land beyond it. The yard, a small patch of mostly brown grass sat empty. A couple of lawn chairs still sat in the middle of it, a tiny fire pit stuck in between them. A sparse white fence bordered the yard, separating it from the rest of his land, untamed trees and fields.

He closed the door behind him and then listened. No sound except a faint breeze, carrying warm air past him. Sweat trickled down his back. The shells in his pockets clacked together softly. He turned the corner to the right side of his house, where the shed lay up against the fence. The shed wasn't huge, big enough to hold his riding lawnmower and other tools.

The right side of the house was as empty as the back, the shed sitting there, the door hanging open. The remnants of the lock laid on the ground, in two pieces. It had been broken.

Ebner crept toward the shed, the flashlight slowly peeking into the interior. He nudged the door open with the tip of the shotgun, and looked inside.

There was nothing but the mower and the normal tools.

No room for something to hide.

STHWOOP.

A sudden noise of movement, something fast on his left, moving toward him and Ebner didn't stop and think he pivoted and fired both barrels of the shotgun. His ears rang from the incredible volume of the gun and before he checked if he hit something he popped open the barrels and ejected the shells, reaching into his pocket and reloading quickly, slamming the barrels shut.

But there was no more noise, and no more movement. He had either killed or wounded or scared off whatever it was, because there wasn't any more of it. His gun reloaded, he scanned the area for something, anything, to see what was left.

He searched over where he had fired, and he saw it, closer than he thought, a bundle of black on the ground. Blood pooled beneath, dark crimson, and Ebner approached it slowly, taking small steps, waiting for any movement at all.

What was it?

As he got close, he saw the black was just a cloak, worn by it. It had folded over, on its side, the cloak covering most of it. Ebner prodded it with his gun, but it didn't move, didn't respond, and he pushed it flat on its back.

It's just a man.

At least that was what Ebner thought for a moment. Some dude dressed in black. It wasn't the first man Ebner had killed—and he was dead, dead as a doornail—but still, the thought of killing didn't make Ebner feel good. But then his light passed over his face—its face. Because whatever it was, wasn't human. The face was something monstrous, split in half from the jaw up past the nose, the eyes still there, but something else now, pupils all black. Where the mouth had been was a gaping maw, some sort of awful tendril shooting out of it, ending in a spike.

"What the fuck are you?" asked Ebner, quietly, but after a few moments the sound of a fire crackling and popping erupted from the man, the thing, whatever it was, and Ebner took a step back out of shock and surprise. He didn't know what the thing was doing, but within a few moments more, the creature burned, burned from inside somehow, the body collapsing in on itself, jets of flame and ash scoring along its skin. A pyre ignited from within, and then the cloak burnt as well. The smell of burning flesh filled the air.

Ebner coughed and turned aside, covering his mouth and nose, but keeping his eyes on the thing as it burnt, both its body and clothes. It burnt hot, and fast, and within thirty seconds, it was gone.

He couldn't believe it. Even the blood was gone, turned to fine ash, and disappeared. He waited in the yard, waiting for something else to come, another of these things, but it didn't happen. He pushed the shed door closed and stuck a stick through the latch to keep it shut for the night.

He walked around the house. His truck was still there, just as he had left it. Nothing else had been touched. Ebner went down the driveway, shotgun still held in his arms, and looked up and down the road. No vehicle parked there.

Either someone had dropped it off, or it had walked to his home.

Ebner went back inside. He looked at the clock. 4 AM. He hadn't looked at it until now. He put the shotgun on the kitchen table and sat down. Didn't bother going back to sleep, knowing it wouldn't take.

He sat and he let his thoughts form on what had happened.

Something had attacked him, in the shape of a man, but with some terrible mouth. It had moved fast, almost fast enough to get him out of nowhere. Only his trigger finger, and knowing it was coming, had saved him. It had walked to his house. It's body was gone, turned to ash in less than a minute after it died.

But it *did* die. The shotgun did the work.

Fuchs had sent it after him. It had been a man, of sorts. A monster that looked like a man. Ebner still didn't want to label it anything besides that. That was enough, for now.

But he needed to know the source. He needed to know the situation.

And after thinking for a few minutes, he bet he knew where he could the answer to both those questions.

He'd find it at Sunny Meadows.

11

He waited until the next night, under cover of dark. A sliver of moon was visible, but it would have to do. Ebner was tired by the time the sun set, even after downing a whole pot of coffee, but it too would have to do. He spent half an hour limbering up, getting his muscles and joints as loose as he could.

Ebner could have driven to the entrance to Sunny Meadows in five minutes on the road, but he didn't know what kind of surveillance they had. He assumed that if there was something hidden there, they would keep an eye on the front gate. So that meant no truck, no vehicles of any kind. He'd have to take it by foot, overland, in the dark, and access Sunny Meadows from the side.

He thought to take a weapon, but brought only a flashlight. It was heavy, and could be a club in a pinch, but if it came to that, Ebner had already lost. This was reconnaissance only. He would have to stay hidden, no matter the cost.

He wore all black. Might not matter in the end, but he wanted to be a shadow. He had a long way to walk in the dark, over land he hadn't taken care of in years.

Ebner left his house as soon as dark had overtaken the sky, walking through his back gate onto his expansive and overgrown property. He cursed his laziness now, in letting it get this bad. The flashlight could show only so much, and he'd be lucky if he didn't turn an ankle accidentally on the way there. The grass had grown tall, with brush growing up past his shoulders along with it. A machete would have been great, but it would have been another thing to carry and slow him down. He'd be traveling over five miles that night, after a long day without sleep, and that wouldn't have been a lot for Ebner forty years ago. Hell, even twenty. But now, five miles felt impossible.

He walked through the dark, keeping his eyes on the ground ahead of him, and his ears open for anything out of the ordinary. But he heard nothing strange, only the wind and the sound of bugs crying out in the night. Ebner hadn't expected those things patrolling his land in the dark, watching out for him, but he didn't know what to expect, not anymore. Not after that thing he killed the night before, not after what had happened to Morris. He hoped that whatever waited for him in Sunny Meadows was normal people in normal houses. He hoped.

But Ebner had never been much on hope.

The evening had cooled from the scorching temperatures of the day, but Ebner still sweat buckets as he hiked, breath coming hot out of his throat and lungs. His heart beat hard within his chest. He'd be sore tomorrow. Well, he hoped.

After an hour of rough hiking he saw the end of his property, and then he saw the wall. Sunny Meadows had a wall built, ten feet high, made of stone, right on the edge of their property. Houses were built up right against it, backyards butted up against the wall. Ebner had never seen the other side, but had watched them build it, in the early days of the development, back before he knew much about Fuchs, or Sunny Meadows.

The wall would be the hardest part, at least physically. When he was young, he probably could have scaled it by hand, without a problem. It wasn't flat, made from jagged rocks stacked haphazardly on top of each other. At least that was the look it was going for. Looked fine to Ebner, but it gave anybody the chance to scale it, with hand and foot holds. There was no barb wire on top, or any other obstacle. It gave the appearance of security, without actually providing any.

At least not against any young person, but Ebner was in his mid-70s, and maybe he could climb that wall, and he might have to, when he would get back over, but he'd worry about that later. He had to get inside first.

Luckily there was a big oak right next to the wall, with several heavy branches that shot right up next to it, close enough for Ebner to get over. Now climbing a tree wasn't that much easier than the wall, but it was doable at his age. Ebner slung the flashlight around his wrist, tying it off tight and letting it dangle as he climbed. The oak sloped gently up and away from the ground, and it was an easy climb up to the first set of branches. He scrambled up to the second set, and then slowly crawled out to the edge of the branch, still plenty thick enough to support his weight. From there, he could look into Sunny Meadows.

He hadn't ever been inside the development. He'd only seen it from the outside, and had no desire to go inside and see row after row of similar homes, built within 5 feet of each other. The thought of being able to reach out his window and touch his neighbor's house felt wrong. But he saw now, into a backyard, and the two backyards adjacent. Of the three of them, only one house had its lights on, the one to his right. Street lights from out in front of the houses cast enough light to see by, if still dim, in the backyard. He scurried out a little farther and put a foot down on top of the wall, and then the other.

Scaling down the wall was much easier, his feet finding the stuck out edges of the rocks quickly. He studied this house, trying to commit it to memory. He wanted to finish back here at the end of his mission. The backyard itself was empty, just a plain plot of grass ending at a concrete lanai with French doors into the house, only darkness visible.

Ebner crouched, creeping toward the house, peering inside. It was dark in there, and he risked using his flashlight to get a better view. He flicked on the light.

The house was empty.

Ebner had sworn that all the houses had sold out in Sunny Meadows. Shouldn't they all be inhabited by now?

Maybe they were snowbirds, and they'd move in after Thanksgiving. Or maybe Fuchs was holding back stock. Who knew? Ebner turned off the light, letting it dangle again. The house to the right was lit up, and he would look.

He didn't know what he was looking for, but he imagined he would know it when he saw it. A white plastic fence separated the two backyards, and Ebner peeked over, seeing his cover from the back windows of the house, and then scaled it as quickly as his old bones would allow. He ducked behind a shed in the backyard, letting himself catch his breath before he peeked back out.

He waited, listening, but heard nothing, and then slowly peeked out. This backyard was decorated with a patio set, landscaping, and the shed he hid behind. They had enclosed the lanai with glass, and the curtains were open, so he could see inside. There were a few lights on, and a man walked across the living room, watching the television within for a minute, and then turning back and disappearing into another part of the house. Ebner watched, and the man never looking out toward him for a moment. How often did Ebner investigate his own shed in the night?

Only when a monster broke it open to lay a trap.

The man appeared again, and this time with a woman. A married couple, Ebner guessed. They looked unspectacular, the man a brunette, the woman a blond, both wearing comfortable clothing. They stood behind their couch and watched whatever was on television. Ebner waited, but they weren't doing anything. Nothing suspicious.

Still, Ebner knew there was something wrong here. There had to be.

He ducked back behind the shed. He did the math in his head. There were hundreds of houses in the development, and he didn't have time to snoop on every one. Maybe this was a bad idea. There had to be a way to figure out—

A distant scream interrupted his thoughts. He peeked back around inside the house. Had they heard it?

The couple both looked in the scream's direction, looking concerned. But then the man gestured to the woman, dismissing it.

Another scream, louder this time. It came from down the street. But Ebner kept his eyes on the couple. They had to have heard it.

The man said something again, and then they both laughed.

Laughed.

Ebner needed to find that scream. He listened for it again, but it was silent now. He would have to go by memory.

He looked back toward the house, and the couple had disappeared out of sight. Ebner moved quickly, crouch walking over to the next fence farther away from his entrance point. He jumped the fence, snagging his pants on the top of it.

He murmured in pain, and found himself in another backyard. Another dark house, and he rubbed at his leg. The pants hadn't been torn. No evidence left behind. With the house empty, he could take his time moving to the next backyard, peeking before he climbed over. It was decorated, showing signs of life. But the house had no lights on. No one was home, or they slept. He doubted the screaming came from it.

Ebner moved to the other side of the yard, peering over again. This house was lit like a Christmas tree, the entire backyard decorated with trellises and lights, the patio adorned with stone and brick pavers. He could see inside the house from there. People moved around inside. A lot of them. At least six loitered in the living room, all circled together.

What the hell was going on? Was this the source of the scream?

And then he saw there were more people in the room, in the center of the circle. Two of them. He didn't recognize the woman, but he knew the man. He had seen him just the other day. Timmy Connor. Had scared him away from Morris' store.

But he didn't look the same now. He had looked afraid that day, after Ebner had put the fear of God into him. His eyes were empty now, glazed over. But that wasn't the first thing Ebner noticed about them.

They were both naked, both the young man and woman. They stared straight ahead, not recognizing any of the circle of people that surrounded them. The circle was six people, three men, three women. Dressed nice enough. Well, they would have been, but their nice clothes were covered in ponchos. Clear, the kind you get at the theme park when it rains.

What the fuck is happening?

But Ebner didn't have time to think it over. The six had told the two something, and they turned slowly and walked, like robots, going farther into the house. Within a few seconds, they'd be beyond Ebner's vision, but then he saw them turn again and realized they were heading upstairs.

He looked up at the second floor of the house. He needed a vantage point, needed to know what the hell was going on in this house. Ebner glanced at the trellis. He could climb it to the roof, and peek inside. Maybe.

Would they hear him? Would they see him?

He didn't know, but it was worth the risk. He needed to know. The entire group filtered upstairs, and then Ebner jumped the fence, feeling a twinge in his hip. He'd be lucky if he could move tomorrow. He moved slowly, closer to the house and trellis, no one inside on the first floor. Testing the trellis, it held his weight, and he climbed.

Soon, his head was level with the second floor, and climbed up and out onto the roof, easing his weight down on the shingles. If he took a wrong step, they would hear him, the roof working as an amplifier. He got as low as he could, circling around the side of the building carefully. He placed each foot with care. There was a window on the north side of the house. He peeked around the edge, and he saw them, and ducked back quickly.

They were all right there, in a bedroom upstairs. But he had seen more than the six and the two. The room was empty, no furniture. Just carpet and bare walls. But not really. Because the entire room was covered in plastic, like you would when renovating a house. His guts ached, a dark thought entering his mind.

He needed to look, but they might see him. They were facing the window, and a mere glance would alert them.

He needed to know.

Ebner slowly peeked, moving a single eye past the corner of the window. Just enough to see. They were all right there, but none of the six looked at him. All of them were fixated on the two nude people who stood with their backs to Ebner. They didn't move, staring straight ahead. He was close enough to hear them talk now.

"What are we waiting for?" asked one.

"They need another minute," said another.

"They'll wake up if we don't give them enough time."

"I'm hungry now."

"You can wait. You fed yesterday."

"Doesn't change that I'm hungry."

"Stop your bickering," said the one that seemed in charge.

He checked his watch, pulling up a sleeve of the poncho.

"Alright, let's start," he said.

And then they all transformed.

And then they fed.

12

The six transformed in front of Ebner's eyes. Their skulls opened up, a vertical line creasing their faces, starting at their chin and splitting up the middle of their face. The skin ripped and bone cracked as they changed, a great maw where their mouth was, pink flesh remolding underneath. Their hands changed, skin mottling into a grotesque gray husk, their fingers shriveling down into razor-sharp points, muscle and bone extending out, the hands bigger than before, widening like a catcher's mitt. If there were more changes, they were hidden beneath their clothes.

But then Ebner saw something extend from their mouths, something he hadn't had time to notice with the thing out on his property, not well. A tendril, pink and wet, formed where their mouth was, the end lined with tiny white teeth.

It happened quickly, their bodies shifting in a minute. Their eyes were still there, but he didn't know how they saw. They were split away from the face, glassy and unused. The tendrils groped the air. Is that how they saw?

But then they fed, and all thoughts of logic and reason left Ebner's mind.

Ebner had seen horrible things in his life, most of them in Vietnam, under the leadership of Lt. Harper. And he'd spent a lot of time locking those thoughts away, keeping them under lock and key. But still, despite that, they escaped from time to time. In dreams, or when triggered by something he saw in his day to day life. And he would spend some time, corral those thoughts again, and shut them away. It was the only way he could live with them. He figured it was what everyone did, when they were confronted with the ugliest aspects of life. And death. They locked them away.

There was no locking this away.

The six creatures converged on the two nude figures, and the tendrils attached to them, the six thin rings of teeth locking onto different parts of the two people, latching onto them like leeches. Blood ran down the man and woman from the different sites, and the monsters fed. They gulped hungrily, and Ebner saw the blood travel through the pink tubes, the flesh warping as the volume of liquid slid down into their gullets. The tendrils found homes on the bodies, one on the stomach, another on the thigh, on the neck, on the breast, three on each person, evenly divided. The six creatures split their share of the feast.

The monstrous sucking noise reached Ebner, and he felt bile rise in his throat, and he swallowed it down. The aching in his gut burned with terror, and he wanted to stop them, try to end this bloodshed, but he only had a flashlight *he should have brought the shotgun, but what were you going to do against six of those THINGS*

The woman fell then, her knees trembling and then giving away, too much blood loss, but none of the tendrils let go, none of those alien mouths were done yet, the three attached to the woman getting closer, getting on all fours to continue to feed. Timmy fell next, thirty seconds later.

Get out of here, Ebner, get out, run run run!

Ebner backed away from the window, realizing the creatures would be full soon, the blood all gone from their victims, and then they'd sense him, and he couldn't fight six of those things, not without a weapon, and panic seized him. He pushed away from the window, back to the trellis, trying to stay quiet, but he didn't know if he could, every footstep a bass drum, and he cut himself on the way down the trellis, they would smell his blood, they would smell his *blood*—

Then he was in the backyard, and he ran, jumping the fence, an empty house, then a house with people, then an empty yard and a way out, and Ebner only thought of his escape then, away from this nightmare, away from whatever those things were. They had fed, and he had heard them gulp down those people's blood, little Timmy's blood, choked down the gullets of those things—

Sweat had soaked through his clothes and his heart beat hard in his chest, and he glanced into the occupied house, and the lights were still on. They were still awake—

Of course they're awake, you know why, you know why—

But they weren't visible, and Ebner climbed their fence and hid behind the same shed as before, taking a breath, peeking out, and they still weren't there, and he wouldn't wait for them, and he moved fast, scaling their other fence, back into the empty backyard, the empty house—

It wouldn't be empty for long, more of them were coming, soon this place would be FULL of them—

The wall surrounding Sunny Meadows stood in front of Ebner, and he didn't hesitate, no time to question if his old body could make the climb, because he scaled, grabbing onto the biggest handholds he could find on the rocky wall, sliding his feet into any slots between the stone.

His chest beat hard, and spots flashed in his eyes as he climbed, his lungs not keeping up with his heart, but he didn't stop, he couldn't stop. Those things were somewhere behind him, and God knows if they had sensed him. He had come to Sunny Meadows because he needed to know, and now he knew, and he climbed away from that terrible knowledge.

His hands and feet slipped away several times, his knuckles scraped and bleeding, but still he went up, his hips and knees screaming with pain, but he didn't stop until he put a foot on top of the wall, and then scrambled to the tree branch, and crawled back to the trunk, his skin scraping against the bark of the oak.

His feet hit the ground, and he sprinted, sure those things were behind him, ready to feast on him, to attach those inhuman mouths to him and drain him of his blood. He ran, the flashlight lighting the little ground it could, his breath coming hot and hard, blood pumping in his ears, his chest rattling with every heartbeat. Ebner pushed himself. He needed to get home, he'd be safe there, but then he fell, his body giving way. He hit the ground, padded somewhat by the long grass.

He laid there, gasping for air, his whole body aching. They were behind him, he knew it, they'd be on him in an instant—

He turned, scanning behind him with the flashlight from his knees.

There was nothing. The wind softly blew past him. The wall of Sunny Meadows stood distant, dim light coming from beyond it.

They hadn't seen him. They weren't chasing.

He sat there, catching his breath. The sweat cooled on him, his shirt and pants sticking to his skin. After a few minutes of not being pursued, Ebner walked back to his house, through his untamed land.

He could breathe again. His body ached, thrumming with pain. It would hurt for days, he knew, but he could deal with pain. The fear lingered, of what he saw, and of what it meant for Fleet.

Thoughts filled his mind as he walked. What had he seen? What were those things, and how many were there? Those two kids were dead, had to be, Timmy Connor and the unknown young woman, their blood suckled from them like a baby at a teat. All of them had changed, changed just like the thing that had come for him in the night. What *was* Sunny Meadows? What was Fuchs?

Answers lingered right at the edge of his grasp as he walked back home. It was still dark by the time he returned, dawn a few hours away. He threw his clothes in the hamper and took a hot shower, letting his mind wander free under the soothing water. He always thought best in the shower, free of distractions. He doubted those things had seen or sensed him, and they wouldn't be pursuing tonight. If they were, he was vulnerable there. He propped the shotgun up against the toilet, within reach if he got an unwelcome visitor. He'd be keeping it within reach from now on.

But none came, and he dried off and dressed, throwing on sweatpants, staying bare-chested. He took the shotgun with him, placing it on the small kitchen table, sitting with it, letting his sore legs rest. He stared at the gun as he pondered, removed from the immediate terror of the situation.

What did he know? Not suspected or thought, but what did he *know*?

Something had attacked him in the night. He had killed it, with a shotgun blast. It burnt away, turned to ash. Before it disappeared, he could see that it wasn't human, mutated in some way.

The six figures he saw in the house in Sunny Meadows were the same. They had fed on two humans, and probably killed them, draining blood from them until they collapsed.

Fuchs owned Sunny Meadows, had built it from the ground up. Fuchs was buying up property. Al Snyder was torn apart on his land, in the night. Morris had been murdered the same, except in his own home.

He knew all that. What did it all mean?

One layer down.

Fuchs owned Sunny Meadows, and he had ordered the deaths of Al and Morris to get the property. Those things had done the killing, probably feeding on them both before tearing them apart.

Second layer down.

Fuchs controlled the creatures and used them to clear the way for his business ventures. Sunny Meadows was their den. But they weren't mindless. Ebner saw them speak.

Fuchs was their boss, not their master. But what were they?

Ebner had never seen anything like it. Had never heard of anything like it. What kind of monster looks like that? Acts like that?

But he knew the answer, had known it as he scrambled through the backyards of Sunny Meadows, as he ran for his life after watching them feed.

Vampires.

The idea was impossible, crazy. Vampires weren't real. Dracula was made up to scare children. Monsters didn't exist. Men did a good enough job at creating horror.

But Ebner believed what he saw, believed in his own two eyes. He wouldn't doubt himself now, *couldn't* anymore.

What creatures drank blood and stayed out at night? Could entrance their victims with a stare? Maybe they didn't have fangs, or talked like Dracula, but they were vampires anyway. Only thing that made sense.

Ebner remembered his lone meeting with Fuchs. The stare. The sunscreen. It all made sense now. Strange behavior in isolation made clear with context.

Fuchs was the lead bloodsucker, the alpha vampire. Sunny Meadows was his den, and Fleet was the first course. The people of Fleet would do more than serve as underlings. They'd serve as meals.

The horrible tension in Ebner's gut had faded slightly as he pondered, but it was back now, worse than ever. Fuchs had taken John under his wing. Was he one of them already? Had Fuchs changed him, turned him into a bloodsucker? The thought was there, and Ebner couldn't dismiss it, couldn't lock it away.

He eyed the shotgun. They could be killed. Didn't need

no silver bullets or holy water neither. Buckshot had done the job. They weren't magic, at least as lead was concerned. Did they have any other tricks up their sleeve? Was Fuchs different from the rest of them?

Dawn was still a couple hours away, but Ebner already knew sleep wouldn't be happening tonight. He doubted a lot of rest was in his future in general. He put on a pot of coffee, and grabbed his gun cleaning kit, and started breaking down the shotgun. Ebner had a feeling he'd be needing it.

But he needed answers about exactly what he faced, and what they could do. It was time for some research.

13

Ebner cruised down Main Street, a trip he'd taken thousands of times in his life, the windows down on his truck, still in second gear. It felt different now. He felt different, now.

He felt *watched*.

Ebner didn't know everyone in Fleet. It felt like a small town, but thirty thousand people lived there, and Ebner certainly didn't know all of them. Don't get it wrong, he knew a lot of them, or at least knew *of* them, whether they be a cousin or an aunt or a nephew of someone he did know.

But he didn't know all of them. But even then, on a normal drive down Main Street, he'd give a small wave or nod to anyone on the sidewalk. Just being friendly. They'd usually return it. Just the way things were in Fleet.

On this drive, he didn't see anyone he recognized. And

he still nodded, still waved, even with that terrible knowledge he had obtained early in the morning, before the sun kissed the land. But it seemed no one nodded or waved back. No smiles, no recognition.

All cold, alien stares, all eyes without humanity.

He looked for any of the people from Sunny Meadows, from the night before, but none of them were here as he scanned every face he saw.

Some of the empty storefronts showed signs of life, with people working inside, either putting new facades up, remodeling, or replacing front panes of glass. All places bought by Fuchs, all being replaced.

Morris's store was closed. Ebner owned it now. Morris had been true to his word, had gotten a new will finalized not two days before his death, all of his belongings passing to Ebner. Ebner didn't know what to do with it all, especially now. He assumed that's why he had been targeted. If his land wasn't big enough, the inheritance had put a bigger bullseye on his back.

Ebner tried to shrug off the looks and glances from the workers inside the storefronts, from the family walking down the street, or ducking into a new shop, one Ebner didn't recognize, but only assumed was owned by Fuchs.

Were they marking him? Keeping an eye on him for Fuchs? Did they know he knew? Did his own eyes betray him?

Ebner didn't think so. His stolid eyes betrayed nothing. But he couldn't know for sure. He didn't know what they could see or sense beyond normal human capability. Could they walk in the sun, as long as they wore their sunscreen? Ebner needed to know.

Fleet's library was downtown, right off of Main Street. It wasn't a big building, and Ebner only went once or twice a year, usually to use a computer for whatever reason. His interests today were a little more broad.

The library wasn't big, a few rooms stacked to the ceiling with books. Ebner wasn't much of a reader, aside from the newspaper and the occasional nonfiction. He'd never braved the stacks.

He sat down at the computer, one of four all bunched together. No one else was there, and he was glad for it. He could manage with the computer, as long as he'd done it before, but the first trip through anything was a struggle. Finding the card catalog on there was easy, and he searched for vampire, and all he got was horror fiction.

How the hell do you switch it to a different category? Ebner tried to click, but it only brought him out of that menu. He tried to click back, and he was lost. Goddamnit, if only—

"Can I help you?" asked a voice from behind him. It was the librarian, and Ebner looked to her name tag. It said Sarah. Sarah was average height, wearing a blouse and black pants, her brown hair tied back in a ponytail. She looked to be in her early 40s, but Ebner didn't know for sure. He didn't know her.

"Hi, uh, Sarah," said Ebner, trying to smile. "Just having some trouble with the card catalog."

"Well, what are you looking for?" asked Sarah.

Ebner scanned her eyes. Could he trust her? She looked genuine, and he saw no sign of sunscreen on her skin. He'd have to. He needed more information. He needed a weakness.

"Vampires," said Ebner.

"Vampires?" asked Sarah. "Are you looking for horror novels?"

"Uh, no," said Ebner. "I want something nonfiction."

"Nonfiction about vampires?" she asked. "You mean, like myths and legends type stuff?"

"Um, if that's what you got," said Ebner.

"Just give me a second," she said. She leaned down and navigated the computer for a second and pulled up a list in moments. "Doesn't look like we have anything like that. A couple libraries nearby have some stuff, if you can wait for an interlibrary loan."

"Uh, sure," said Ebner. "Put me down for whatever they got."

"I need your library card," said Sarah.

"Right," said Ebner, reaching into his pocket and pulling out his wallet. It was in there somewhere. He fished through it, pulling apart layers of cards for everything, for grocery stores, old insurance cards, wait, *there it was*—

"I still need to do some business on here," said Ebner.

"I can go take care of this at my desk," said Sarah. "Come see me when you're ready." She left again, and Ebner waited for her to leave before he continued.

He hadn't expected much from the library, to be honest, especially one like Fleet's. Small town library won't have much on vampires. But Morris had told him that YouTube had videos for everything, even stuff that people said was fake.

Ebner searched for YouTube and found it, and searched for "vampire" on there. Ebner looked down the list. Nothing but references to movies and video games. He needed the real stuff.

"Real vampire" got him nothing but frauds. He'd seen the real thing, in the flesh, had looked Fuchs right in the eye. None of these people had it. They just wanted attention.

He needed to know more about them, actual information about real vampires. More than that, he needed to know their weaknesses. Shotguns were all well and good, but a shotgun wasn't going to do the trick against hundreds of them.

Who knew how to kill vampires?

Ebner searched "real vampire hunter" next, and got a long list of results, but definitely on the right track. But there were frauds in here as well, people who pretended to be a vampire hunter for fun. They weren't the real thing. He could see it in their eyes they hadn't killed anyone, certainly not vampires.

Ebner scrolled through videos, staring at each person's eyes. He would know it when he saw it.

Nothing.

Nothing.

Nothing.

Then he saw it. He knew it right away, the same look he saw in the mirror. A look of sadness, and danger, and potential.

Her eyes were emerald green, bright, and they contained it all, and he knew she was legitimate. Her hair burned a fiery red, her cheekbones sharp enough to cut through shoe leather. She wore an amulet around her neck, big and circular, the same color as her eyes.

The video wasn't about vampires, though. The video's title said "Leprechauns - No Luck, More Than Myth". Ebner clicked through to her profile, and she had dozens of videos, all about different mythical creatures and monsters. "The Monster Hunter, Anastasia Wraithwhite" was her name, and those same eyes burned at him from every single video. Ebner scrubbed through the videos, looking for anything referencing vampires.

"Werewolves Sighted in Idaho"

"Mermen in the Keys, Fact or Fiction"

"Real Demon Summoning in Kansas!"

"C'mon, c'mon," said Ebner. "It's damn vampires, for God's sakes." Finally, he found one, one of her oldest videos. "Close Call with a Vampire". The video wasn't long, only four minutes. Most of her videos were close to twenty. It probably didn't bode well.

He clicked on it, putting on the headphones lying next to the computer.

Anastasia spoke to the camera. She sat in what looked to be her office. She was dressed conservatively, with a white collared blouse and black pants. Her muscular shoulders bulged at the fabric of her blouse. Another sign of a hunter. She was not soft.

She introduced herself and the channel, and asked for subscriptions and likes, and other buzzwords Ebner didn't recognize.

"C'mon, get to the good stuff," he murmured.

"I've gotten a lot of requests about vampires," said Anastasia. "And I understand the requests. Vampires are a scourge to the wide world. But a lack of a video is only because I lack the information I need. Vampires camouflage so neatly among us in the human world, it is often quite difficult to track down sightings and investigate. I don't do videos on subjects I don't have complete information, or information

I don't have confidence in. I can share this, my only experience with what I suspect was a vampire." She paused, for dramatic effect. "I had heard reports of a vampire in uptown Manhattan, who had been seen perusing upscale restaurants. My theory is that vampires are often wealthy, because they've had long lives to accrue wealth. But I went, and began going to different restaurants for every meal. I dressed down, to try and stay hidden, but the beast still found me. I don't know how it spotted me, or saw my suspicion, but as I walked to the restroom, a man cornered me, a man with blond hair and strange, hollow eyes." She paused now, but not for effect. She had remembered those eyes, and the effect they had on her. "He tried to hypnotize me. If he had succeeded, I doubt I would be here. But the amulet saved me. As I fell under his spell, it sensed the danger and alerted me. I woke up, standing there, the man looking confused. He couldn't believe it, I suspect. But then he was gone, in an instant, while I blinked. The reports died away, as he most likely moved shop, to some other place to feed."

Only another minute left in the video.

"I believe he was a vampire. But I've never encountered either him or any of his kind again. Maybe they know me now and do their best to avoid me. But I'm still looking for information, and will update with a new video if I ever encounter more. If you have any information, please message me."

She ended the video with more platitudes, but Ebner was already trying to find a way to message her. He needed an account. *Fuck.* Ebner hated making more accounts, but he found his way to it, and gave them the information they wanted, even if they didn't need half of it. He just needed to message this lady. She needed to know what was happening in Fleet.

He finally got to the place he wanted, and he slowly typed, hunting and pecking.

Dear Ms Wraithwhite,

My name is Ebner Graves and I live in Fleet, Texas. The town is being overrun by vampires. Oskar Fuchs is the name of the gentleman who I believe is the leader of them. I need your help. He is buying up the town and feeding residents to his followers. I am the only one who knows, I believe. I saw them transform and feed with my own two eyes, and they have killed my best friend. Morris Stevens is his name. You should be able to find the police report online. I do not have regular access to a computer, but my phone number is 555-555-5555. Please contact me as soon as possible. I intend to stop them.

Truly,
Ebner Graves

He hit the send button, and waited for it to confirm. He didn't have much more information, but he had at least sent for help. But there was no guarantee she would get the message, or come to Fleet. He would have to rally local forces. Sheriff Hicks was no fan of Fuchs. Maybe Ebner could get him to help.

Ebner closed everything and went to the desk, where Sarah waited for him with a smile.

"Did you find what you needed?" she asked, handing

him back his library card. He returned her smile.

"I hope so."

14

The Fleet Sheriff's Office was within walking distance of the library, but Ebner drove. His legs still ached from his trip to Sunny Meadows.

There were only a few cars in the parking lot, but Hicks' big SUV was parked there, and that's the one person he wanted to talk to. The office was relatively small, a tiny outpost.

"Is Sheriff Hicks free?" asked Ebner, to the deputy at the desk, but Hicks answered before the deputy had a chance.

"Come on in, Ebner," said Hicks, yelling at him from his open office, only ten feet away. Ebner walked in. "Shut the door behind you." Ebner closed the glass door, Hicks' name painted on.

Ebner sat down in the worn pleather chair in front of

Hicks' small desk, covered in loose stacks of paper and files. A monitor sat on the corner, mostly forgotten. Hicks drank from a giant thermos. Ebner knew it was coffee, enough to fuel a jet.

"How you doing, Ebner?" asked Hicks, leaning back in his chair.

"Could be better, I suppose," said Ebner.

"Never a lie," said Hicks. "Wife tells me it's a frame of mind, you know. If you're happy, you're happy. But the grass is always greener."

"You find any leads about Morris?" asked Ebner.

Hicks met his eyes. "No."

"Nothing?" asked Ebner.

"No," said Hicks. "Crime scene guy did his due diligence, but there was nothing there, at least nothing that Morris didn't put there himself. No foreign DNA, no tracks, no trace elements of anything out of the ordinary. Morris' blood had trace amounts of alcohol in it—"

"Morris drank three beers a night for the past forty years," said Ebner. "Always three."

"That's what we figured," said Hicks. "But no other narcotics or drugs in his system. Also no sign of animal presence. No fur, and the wounds came back negative for all known attack markings."

Ebner stared at Hicks. "How do you explain that?" asked Ebner.

Hicks raised his eyebrows and licked his lips, pursing them. "I don't," said Hicks. "I'm closing the case."

"What do you mean, you're closing the case?" asked Ebner.

"There is no evidence, Ebner," said Hicks. "Nothing.

Zilch. What am I supposed to do? Interrogate everyone in town?"

"Fuchs—"

"Fuchs has an airtight alibi," said Hicks. "A dozen people can corroborate he was busy that night."

"I never said it was him directly," said Ebner. "He sent something there to kill Morris."

"Some*thing*?" asked Hicks. "Something like what?"

Ebner eyed Hicks. Could he trust him? Ebner took a deep breath, exhaled.

"Do you believe in vampires?" asked Ebner.

"Vampires?" asked Hicks, half-smiling. "Like Dracula? Twilight?"

"Immortal creatures that drink blood to survive."

"You're serious."

"Yes."

"Are you telling me you think Fuchs is a vampire?" asked Hicks.

"Yes," said Ebner. "Not just him. Sunny Meadows is a vampire den. All the residents are vampires."

Hicks stared at him. "All of them?"

"Probably," said Ebner. "I can't be sure, but I'm guessing you don't live there unless you've been turned."

"You feeling alright, Ebner?" asked Hicks.

"I told you, I've felt better," said Ebner. "But I'm not crazy, if that's what you're asking."

"You've been under a lot of stress lately," said Hicks. "Maybe it might be better if you let this all go."

"Let it go?" asked Ebner. "How the hell am I supposed to do that?"

"Go home, and relax," said Hicks. "Do some chores

around the house. Read. Think things through a little."

"They're Goddamn vampires, Bart," said Ebner. "I'm not crazy, and I'm not stressed out, whatever the fuck that means. They've been creeping around my house at night, trying to lure me outside, just like they did to Al. Fuchs wants my land, and it's a lot easier to get it if I'm dead."

"Creeping around your house?" asked Hicks.

"Yes," said Ebner. "They've—" He stopped himself. He couldn't tell the Sheriff he killed one. Or that he'd been trespassing at Sunny Meadows. "They're trying to get me the same way."

"You haven't filed any reports with us, have you?" asked Hicks.

"No," said Ebner. "What am I supposed to say? I keep hearing noises in the night? I'm not gonna have a sheriff come out for that."

Hicks grabbed a pencil and wrote something.

"What you writing?" asked Ebner.

"Just some notes, Ebner," said Hicks.

"Have you talked to Fuchs, Bart?" asked Ebner. Hicks paused, glancing up at Ebner, and then back down.

"We had a chat," said Hicks. "He came here, into the office. Sat down. Had a reasonable discussion."

Ebner's gut soured. It was too late.

"You're one of them, now," said Ebner.

"I'm not one of anything, Ebner," said Hicks. "We had a nice, sensible discussion, and Fuchs changed my mind on a few things. That's it."

"He told you to drop Morris' case," said Ebner.

"He told me no such thing," said Hicks, finally looking up again into Ebner's eyes. Ebner read him, trying to see if he'd been turned, if he was one of those filthy bloodsuckers. Ebner didn't see it, but he hadn't seen it earlier, either. Something was wrong there, though, something Ebner had overlooked. "We just talked through some things, and a lot clicked in place. I had disliked him and I hadn't really talked to him, not really. He made things clear."

A certain airiness had entered Hicks' voice, and Ebner realized it now, remembered his own meeting with Fuchs. Remembered the two victims in Sunny Meadows. They'd put up no resistance, had done exactly as ordered. Ebner looked to Hicks' eyes, and something was missing from them.

Free will, Ebner. That's what's missing. Fuchs has sucked all the choice out of him.

Hicks just kept on talking. "You should really give him another chance, Ebner. He made some good points, about how he's going to bring a lot of new jobs to the area, and you know, I have to worry about more than just Fleet. I have to worry about the whole county. He even told me he might find a place for me and the wife in Sunny Meadows. We've been thinking about selling the old homestead for a few years now anyway, and he laid out all the benefits of living there. It seemed mighty attractive—"

Ebner stopped listening, but Hicks kept on talking, reciting a list of bullet points implanted in his head. Put there by Fuchs, when Fuchs had marched in here and looked Hicks right in the eyes. And now Hicks was smart to Ebner's info on Fuchs. About Sunny Meadows, about his thoughts on vampires.

Stupid, Ebner, stupid. Now you've lost your advantage.

Maybe not.

Hicks still talked. "And man, you don't know how great it'll be to have a Shake Shack in town—"

"Maybe you're right," said Ebner.

"What?" asked Hicks, his eyes slightly glazed.

"Maybe I have been under a lot of stress," said Ebner. "I've lost a lot of friends lately, you know?"

"Yeah, Ebner," said Hicks. "That's what I'm saying. Must not be easy."

Ebner pictured William's face in his mind. Thought of that moment when William told him about his diagnosis. A tear formed in the corner of his eye and rolled down his cheek. He wiped it away, but waited, letting Hicks see it.

"It's been tough," said Ebner. "And I've been watching a lot of YouTube videos, and they're all talking about how vampires are taking over small communities, and maybe—maybe I just thought it was happening here too. But it's crazy, y'know? Fuchs isn't a vampire. Sunny Meadows is just a planned community."

Hicks' face softened. "It's alright, Ebner," said Hicks. "None of us blame you, you know? You've been through a lot, and have lived here a long time. Change is hard. And you push yourself real hard, and at your age? You should be enjoying life. Maybe rethink Fuchs' offer. It's real generous, and with that kind of money, you could do anything, go anywhere. Retire to Tahiti. Stare at bikini girls on the beach all day."

Ebner forced a smile, tried to make it as a genuine as possible. "That's an idea," said Ebner, and Hicks laughed, his boisterous laugh filling the small office. Sounded real to Ebner, but he didn't know anymore. But maybe if he changed course, Hicks wouldn't report back the vampires to Fuchs.

Maybe Ebner would still have that small advantage. 'Cause he needed all he could get.

"I'm sorry, Bart," said Ebner, rubbing his hands together, staring Hicks in the eye. "Feel like I wasted your time over nothing."

"Oh, don't say that," said Hicks. "I'm here to help, and if you're a little more clearheaded than you were coming in, then I've done my job. You're a pillar of the community, Ebner. It's what everyone thinks. Your opinion is important. It holds sway. Just want you on the right team, is all."

"No, I understand," said Ebner. His heart burned, burned hard, as he pushed down the rage. He wanted to drag Hicks over his messy desk and beat the shit out of him in his own office, for being so weak, for being swallowed up by that monster's hypnosis.

But he forced it down. He didn't think it'd work, didn't think you could just beat it out of someone. Maybe if he killed Fuchs, maybe the hypnosis would break.

But Ebner didn't think it'd be hypnosis for very long. Eventually he'd turn Hicks. Turn all the cops in the county, probably. With the law on his side, Fuchs could do what he wanted. Take things by force.

Ebner saw it now. Fuchs' plan was taking root. Fuchs knew this would all happen, and soon he'd have complete control over Fleet, and then spread out from there.

Ebner had to stop him, no matter the cost. But he didn't know how he'd do it, not anymore.

He got up and extended a hand toward Hicks, who took it and shook it. No difference in his handshake. Ebner left without a glance back. He hoped his dog and pony show would keep Hicks from telling Fuchs what he knew.

As he drove home, back down Main Street, he nodded and waved to everyone he saw walking down the street. More than usual. He still felt their eyes. He still felt watched.

His phone was ringing when he got home, and he hurried inside to answer it.

Maybe it's Ms. Wraithwhite. Maybe she can help.

He answered the phone.

"Hello?" he said. Ms. Wraithwhite's voice was not who answered. It was Joanna.

"Hi, Ebner," she said. "I know this is short warning, but could you come over? We need to talk."

"Talk about what?" asked Ebner.

"About John." She paused, but Ebner could hear her breath. "About Fuchs."

15

Ebner got back in his truck and drove over. Joanna called *him*. It had to be bad for Joanna to call him.

There hadn't always been the distance between them. At first, they were close. They were similar people, in a lot of ways, and neither of them saw the other as an enemy. Joanna was a friend for William, a smokescreen to cover for their relationship. Ebner, to Joanna, was a best friend, someone who loved William, who'd do anything for him, support him to the end.

Things only got complicated when they both realized that the other would always be competition for William, for his attention, for his time, for his *love*. Because Joanna knew William loved Ebner, even if she didn't *know* it was romantic. And whatever type it was, it was something from

William she wasn't getting.

And maybe that wasn't mature of them. Maybe they would have been happier if they all knew the score, and managed their expectations more reasonably. It's possible they could have worked something out, together, instead of slowly negotiating it all in the dark, feeling around without a light or a clue.

None of them had that vocabulary, though, or the capability. They both loved William, and they both wanted all of him. But they also loved him so much that having some of him was enough.

But they respected each other, even at the worst of times. They knew that each were dedicated to William, to doing whatever it took for him. And no matter how much jealousy that might arise, or hurt feelings, or even disdain, they knew William was safe with the other.

It was enough.

John complicated things. Ebner saw John a lot, enough for him to be Uncle Ebner for a large portion of John's life. But John saw him as more of a parent than an uncle, sometimes more than his own mother, and it tore Joanna apart. And Ebner tried to push John away, to force him on his mother, but it mostly didn't work. John controlled his own orbit, and often he chose Ebner before he chose William or Joanna, even if Ebner didn't always show that affection.

But he loved John, just like he loved William, and that ended up being enough for Joanna. She never pulled the pin on that grenade.

THWACK
THWACK
THWACK

A loud noise greeted Ebner as he got out of his truck at Joanna's place. He followed the noise to the backyard, where he found Joanna chopping firewood, her form clean, bringing the axe down in a wide arc, from high above her head, cutting through piece after piece. Will and Jo had never replaced the wood stove that heated their house in winter, and so they would keep a stack of firewood stocked up. Even at her age, Ebner saw the strength in Joanna's shoulders. William had a *type*.

"Think you'd replace that wood stove by now," said Ebner. Jo turned, saw him, and finished her last strike. *THWACK* went the piece of wood, split in two, and then she put the axe aside, leaned up against the pile of wood, already building for the coming winter.

"Too late for that," said Joanna. "Been burning wood in that stove for this long. Don't think I'll stop now."

"Fair enough," said Ebner.

"Let's go inside," said Joanna. "I need some water."

Ebner followed her through the back door. She grabbed some water for herself and got him some as well. They sat at the kitchen table, the same places as last time. They both were creatures of habit.

"I talked to Fuchs, Ebner," said Joanna. She took a long drink of water, gulping it down, and then meeting his eyes, their mirror stares. "I don't like him, Ebner. There's something wrong with his eyes. We have to get John away from him. You were right."

"I don't know how we can," said Ebner. "I—" The conversation with Hicks flashed in his mind. Hicks was in Fuchs' pocket. Was Jo in there as well? Was everyone in Fleet a trap laid by Fuchs?

But he couldn't have this conversation without telling her. Even if it made him sound crazy.

"Can I trust you, Jo?" asked Ebner, his voice hard and sad.

"Trust is a hard thing to come by, these days," she said. Another drink of water. "You can trust me, but the asking makes me more worried than anything."

"You're not wrong," said Ebner. "What I'm going to tell you is going to sound crazy. Especially coming from me. But that don't make it any less true. And the knowing is the only advantage I have on Fuchs at the moment."

"Well, what is it?" asked Joanna.

"Fuchs—Fuchs isn't human," said Ebner. "Al Snyder, he got torn apart out in his front yard. Hicks had said it was wolves, back before Fuchs took control of him. But why on Earth would Al go out into his yard if he knew there were wolves? It wasn't wolves. It was a vampire that did it. Or vampires."

"Vampires?" asked Joanna.

"Just hold on," said Ebner. "I mention Al because Fuchs tried the same for me. Sent someone to make noise outside the house at night, except I knew their game, and I was ready. I killed 'em."

"You killed them?" asked Joanna.

"Yeah, with my shotgun. Saw a shape coming at me from the dark, and I pulled the trigger. At first, thought it was man. But it wasn't. It's face was wrong, split in half, opened up, with some sort of tendril sticking out. But its body burnt away, self destructed before I could take a look."

"Ebner—"

"Just wait. I went to Sunny Meadows, in the night. Snuck

around. Saw a group of them feeding. They killed Timmy Connor and some girl, don't know her name. I saw them change, in front of my eyes. They drank those two kid's blood, drained them dry. Fuchs is a vampire, Joanna, and so is everyone in Sunny Meadows. It's more than just some planned development. It's a vampire den, a safe haven."

Joanna's face changed then, from confusion and question marks to concern and fear, some switch flipped inside of her.

"You sure about this?" asked Joanna. "You're right, this doesn't sound like you."

"I saw it with my own two eyes," said Ebner. "You looked into Fuchs' eyes, didn't you? What did you feel?"

Joanna stared at him, those unyielding eyes showing some give. She shook her head, thinking of a word. "Hopeless," she said, finally. "It felt like it was robbing me of everything worth something. All my hopes, my dreams, my thoughts and feelings. My memories of William. When I stared at him, it felt hopeless."

"But you got away," said Ebner.

"My phone rang," said Joanna. "While we were talking."

"Car backfired," said Ebner. "When I talked to him. He can hypnotize people. Entrance them, enslave them. That's where Hicks is. He got lost in there, and whatever's walking around isn't Hicks anymore. He goes to it right away, if he can't buy people out. I turned down his offer, and he tried to brainwash me."

"I don't know, Ebner. Vampires?" asked Joanna. "I thought they were bats. I thought sunlight burned them. I talked to Fuchs in broad daylight."

"He wears sunscreen. So does any of his kind that go

outside in the day," said Ebner. "But they still don't like it. I don't know. Myths and legends get started for a reason, but it's a game of telephone, over the years. Certain facts get misheard, or misunderstood. They change shape, when they feed. Who knows what they can do?"

"John is seeing Fuchs all the time," said Joanna. "Most about every day, now."

"That's what I was worried about," said Ebner. "He hasn't returned my calls since Morris' funeral. He doesn't want to hear anything negative about him. He thinks I'm trying to undermine his decisions."

"I mean, that's what I thought too," said Joanna. "It wouldn't be the first time."

"I've always tried to do the best for him," said Ebner. "Most of the time it was Will's ideas, anyway. John just listened to me, so I was the one to tell him."

"Damn it, Will," said Joanna. "He always had to be the good guy."

"He was good at it," said Ebner. "I wish he was still here. Could use his help right about now."

"If wishes were horses, beggars would ride," said Jo. "Will's gone. We're all that's left. We have to help him. We have to get him away from Fuchs."

"I don't know how," said Ebner. "He won't listen to me anymore. Maybe with you—"

"I tried to talk to him the other day," said Joanna. "After my talk with Fuchs. Like you said, he wouldn't hear any of it. He wants to sell the shop. Fuchs made him an offer for a position in his company, overseeing the development of all his Fleet property."

"Fuck," said Ebner. "At this point, I don't care about the

shop. I care about John."

"Are you sure that everyone living in Sunny Meadows is one of them?" asked Joanna. She couldn't say the word.

"I don't rightly know," said Ebner. "But it's what my gut tells me is the truth, and it usually steers me right. It's self contained, walled in, has its own security. All the privacy in the world. If there are people living in there who haven't been turned yet, it probably won't be long until they are. Hicks talked about moving there. I reckon it's how Fuchs gets people prepared for the turn. Bring them closer and closer, until they don't know the difference, and aren't so shocked when they're confronted with the truth."

Joanna took a deep breath then, holding it, and then letting it out slowly. She took another long drink of water. "John is doing more than selling the store. He told me Fuchs had offered him a place in Sunny Meadows. A new house, fully furnished."

"When's he moving in?" asked Ebner.

Joanna stared at him. "Yesterday. He moved yesterday."

16

It's too late. It's too late.

The only thought that circulated in Ebner's mind is that they had already lost John. Ebner had been busy scouting out Sunny Meadows, and he hadn't realized that John was already in danger, already had decided. He'd assumed that John would tell him, would at least let him know that he was selling.

Ebner drove down to the shop. If John wasn't there, he'd go to his house, and then into Sunny Meadows itself. He would find him. There was still time. He could pull John back from the brink. With Joanna's support, they could convince John to change his mind. They could save John, and they could save Fleet.

John's old truck wasn't there, and Ebner cursed, but there

was a new truck there, factory stickers still on it, shining and white. Ebner had a suspicion, and he pulled in to the parking spot next to it, his beat up old truck looking like an antique next to the shining thing.

The door on the sign said closed, but Ebner knew better, and he pushed his way inside, the door not locked. Ebner heard the clatter, and he knew immediately John was inside and then he saw him. His back was to him, dismantling a piece of equipment, his hands black with grease.

"Sorry, we're closed," said John without looking back. "Can't help you today."

"I certainly hope that's not true," said Ebner. "Because I desperately need it."

John turned. "Ebner," said John. "Didn't think you'd be coming around anymore."

"Why is that, John?" asked Ebner. "Given up on me?"

"No," said John. "You're stubborn. I didn't expect you to change your mind."

"Change my mind about what?" asked Ebner.

"About Oskar's offer," said John. "You've refused to listen to reason, time after time, and I thought this wasn't any different."

Ebner walked closer, studying John's eyes. They looked the same. John still talked about business. Maybe there was still time. Maybe Fuchs hadn't made him into a monster yet. The tension in Ebner's guts eased a little.

"I heard you moved into Sunny Meadows," said Ebner.

"Sort of," said John. "Only some of my stuff. Haven't slept there yet."

"Thought you'd at least call me to tell me you were going to sell," said Ebner.

"Why would I do that?" asked John. "So you can yell at me some more? Treat me more like a child?"

Ebner shook his head. "Because it's the right thing to do, John. Because you know that I care about this place. Because I sold it to you when you had no other options."

"That's not true," said John. "I had plenty of options. Just none left in Fleet."

"You don't have to do this, John," said Ebner.

"Why are you still doing this?" asked John, stopping what he was doing, staring at Ebner. "I've made up my mind."

"Why am I still doing this?" asked Ebner. "That's a hell of a question. Because I love you, John. Because I was a young man once, and I made some bad decisions, and I don't want you to do the same."

John's eyes wavered, for just a second, but they hardened again.

"You always treated me like a kid," said John. "I know exactly what I'm doing. Oskar treats me like a partner. Like an adult. He didn't trick me, Ebner. He made me an offer, I considered it, and I took it. If you were smart, you'd do the same."

Ebner took a short breath. He had to tell him. It was the only way.

"You have to get out now, John," said Ebner. "Fuchs, all his people in Sunny Meadows. They're not human. They're something else. Vampires, or something like it. They're monsters. They killed Al, and Morris, and Timmy Connor, and some poor girl, and God knows who else. And if you stay there for too long, you'll be next."

"Ebner—"

"Listen to me! I may be some stubborn old man, clinging

to the past, but I'm not crazy. I'm sorry for how I've acted, how I treated you, but this isn't about Fleet, or the shop! You are in danger! Not just you, but your soul!"

"Ebner, please go," said John, staring into his eyes. Ebner stared back. A bead of sweat slid down John's face, and Ebner looked to it, reflexively. It was stained with white, and Ebner saw it now, his face slightly glowing, the light from the overhead fluorescents shining off his face.

Sunscreen.

He had been wrong, his eyes' judgment wrong.

Ebner's stomach dropped, and he couldn't breathe, taking a step back, then two. He forced air into his lungs, a deep gasping breath. He doubled over.

"You okay, Ebner?" asked John, reaching out with a hand.

"Don't touch me," said Ebner. "Keep your filthy hands away from me."

"I—"

"How could you?" asked Ebner. "How could you become—become one of those things?"

John dropped his hand, his face quiet and undisturbed.

"Do you think the decision was hard, Ebner?" asked John. "Have you considered for even a moment what it means? All my life, I've just wanted to be able to take care of myself. Not have to lean on other people. But what have I done, for the entirety of my adult life? Get a job because of you and Dad. Buy this place, with Dad's money. Have to do odd jobs to make end's meet, when the shop stopped making money. Struggling, every single day. Never being good enough. Never not worrying about paying my bills. You and Dad telling me time after time that hard work pays off. Just keep grinding, John, and you'll get there. Well, *there* never showed up. *There* was always out of my grasp, Ebner. I worked myself to death, and never showed any sign of progress. All I got was ulcers."

"This is different, John, and you know it," said Ebner.

"Is it?" asked John. "Oskar shows up, and makes an incredible offer. But not only that, he gave me control. I get to decide how to shape Fleet for the future. I get to build a life, a real life, with control. With money. With power."

"You're one of those things, now, John," said Ebner. "There ain't no going back."

John's eyes burned. "Do you remember how Dad looked at the end, Ebner? I'm sure you do."

Will's emaciated body flashed in Ebner's mind, his flesh withered down to a skeleton with skin, the man he loved worn down to a nub. The cancer and the treatment took everything from him.

"I'll never be sick, ever again," said John. "I don't need to sleep. I'm never tired. You have no idea. I feel like Superman. I'll never die, Ebner. Ever. I will never wither away to nothing like Dad did. I will never have to face something like that. And the cost? Wearing some sunscreen on sunny days. Easy price. I'll pay it every time."

"It's not the only cost," said Ebner, steel in his voice. "I saw them feed, John. I have a feeling that ain't optional."

John shrugged. "Everything has a cost, Ebner," said John. "It's not a heavy one."

"What about those people?" asked Ebner. "That blood has to come from somewhere. From someone."

"They volunteer, Ebner," said John. "They line up happily to be of service. They love it."

"Are you sure about that?" asked Ebner. "Are you sure

they're not just hypnotized?"

John shrugged again. Ebner couldn't recognize him anymore. The mask John wore when Ebner first came in was gone, replaced by this thing, whatever Fuchs had given him.

"That's something you and Dad never told me," said John. "You never prepared me for it. It doesn't surprise me, really. Your lives were easy, born into times of plenty. Plenty enough to go around for everyone. No need to struggle, or claw. A machining job at a factory was enough to live on, to retire on! But it's not like that anymore, Ebner. There isn't enough to go around, not anymore. If you want to live, if you want to succeed, if you want to *thrive*—you have to take. You have to fight, and claw, and *dig* for every last piece. There is no coasting. There is no time for rest. You push every day, as hard as you can, and anyone that gets close, you trip them up, you knock them down."

He stared hard at Ebner, half smiling.

"So nothing much has changed for me, Ebner," said John. "If I want to succeed, someone else has to suffer. So be it. I didn't choose the world I was born into."

"But you chose this," said Ebner. "You chose this horror."

"That's where you're wrong, Ebner," said John. "This isn't horror. This is perfection. This is the dream. Imagine, Ebner—just imagine. Imagine if Oskar had come around just a year ago, instead of now. When Dad was still alive. Still fighting."

"No—"

"He'd still be here, Ebner. The cancer would be gone. He'd be strong, and healthy, and live forever."

"And live with that curse forever," said Ebner. "Turn into some kind of bloodsucking freak."

"You wouldn't say that if you had it," said John. "If you knew what it felt like—you'd be down on your knees, begging Oskar. You would sign on the dotted line, no questions asked."

Ebner's heart ached, and he felt tears well in the corners of his eyes. He wiped them away.

"It's not too late, Ebner," said John. "You still have time. Oskar is a patient man, a forgiving man. Admit you were wrong, accept his offer, and you can be one of us. He'll welcome you with open arms. Imagine it, Ebner. No more creaky bones. You can be as strong as you were when you were young. No more aging. No more death."

"Fuchs isn't a man, anymore," said Ebner. "And neither are you. And dying is a part of life, John."

"Not anymore," said John. "If you'll excuse me, I've got more work to do. But please, reconsider. There's still time."

John turned, back to working on disassembling the equipment.

Ebner stared at him, trying to find words, searching for something inside him, but Ebner had been right when he came in.

It was too late.

17

Ebner stepped out into the light, his eyes adjusting to the sun. He needed to talk to Joanna, needed to tell her about John. She didn't deserve the same shock he got—

"Imagine meeting you here," said a voice, and Ebner knew it right away, turning to see Fuchs, his eyes still adjusting.

"You son of a bitch," said Ebner and swung at Fuchs before he could barely see him, swinging as hard as he could.

He hit nothing. His fist flew through empty air, and he had to catch himself from falling over, his knees complaining. He blinked, his eyes used to the light again, and turned to swing again. Fuchs stood there, watching him.

"You cannot hit me, Mr. Graves," said Fuchs. "No matter how hard you swing."

Ebner charged at him and swung again, his heart filled with rage and sadness. Fuchs moved, faster than Ebner could see, and Ebner hit nothing.

Ebner fell this time, his foot slipping, and he crashed to the sidewalk. He laid there, the dirty concrete in front of his face. His knee ached from smashing into the ground, and his heart pounded in his chest. He forced himself up, and Fuchs was there, waiting for him.

"Please stop this," said Fuchs. "You look silly."

"Go fuck yourself, leech," said Ebner, spitting at him. Fuchs moved, faster than Ebner could track.

"That won't work either, Mr. Graves."

"Go to hell. You're a killer."

"That's awfully hypocritical of you, Mr. Graves," said Fuchs. "I know you've killed yourself. More than once, most likely."

"They tore Morris apart in his living room," said Ebner. "Ain't no way for a man to die."

"I didn't order that," said Fuchs. "I had ordered a warning. No violence. The two men I sent were overzealous."

"You're lying," said Ebner.

"I am not," said Fuchs. "I don't lie, Mr. Graves. I'm well past the need for dishonesty. The two men responsible for Morris' death were punished."

"Punished how?" asked Ebner.

"They're dead," said Fuchs. "I killed them myself."

Ebner eyed him. Fuchs' hollow eyes stared back, but Ebner didn't detect a lie. But he couldn't be sure. He couldn't be sure of anything anymore.

"And the man outside my house?" asked Ebner.

"Meant to frighten you," said Fuchs. "I'm frankly impressed you were fast enough to kill him. But he was no great loss. He was chosen because he would not be missed. But he would not have killed you. The same with your sojourn into Sunny Meadows. Any one of my children could have killed you then, but I told them to let you go, even if I don't like people discovering the truth without proper context."

"Proper context?" asked Ebner. "You mean, you softening up their heads first?"

"When you have startling news for someone, do you just tell them right away? No. You break it to them slowly, to soften the blow."

Ebner only stared. "I'm more of a rip the bandaid off type of guy."

"Somehow I'm not surprised."

"What about Al?" asked Ebner.

"I take responsibility for that," said Fuchs. "One of my children went feral."

"Feral?" asked Ebner. "So you are animals."

"Anyone with power can be dangerous," said Fuchs. "So I only bestow it to ones I believe are worthy of it. My judgment is not always perfect. But I correct my mistakes."

"Well, you'll have to forgive me if I tell you to rot in Hell."

"Please, Mr. Graves, we don't have to be enemies. I want you on our side."

"I don't want to be one of you things," said Ebner. "Even after you've corrupted John. Turned him against his will, warped his mind."

Fuchs laughed again, that alien sound Ebner had heard on his porch.

"You think this is funny?" asked Ebner. "These are people's lives."

"I'm laughing at you, Mr. Graves," said Fuchs, the smile disappearing from his face as quickly as it appeared. "I'm laughing at you. Sometimes, I forget what a typical person thinks about us."

"You mean human?" asked Ebner.

"I'm guessing you're referring to my ability to hypnotize," said Fuchs. "It's of limited use, and only to those who are easily suggestible. If you're thinking I used it to alter John's opinion of me, or made him want to sell, to become one of us, that is ridiculous."

"That isn't the John I knew in there—"

"That's certainly correct," said Fuchs. "The John in there is someone who saw what they wanted and took it. They didn't rest on their laurels, trapped in a town by their father. And regardless of what you think I did, Mr. Graves, John chose his own fate. You may disagree if you'd like about what I am, about what we are, but he made the decision. He chose to be turned."

"Yeah, after you forced him into the situation, put pressure—"

"He would be dead, Mr. Graves," said Fuchs. "You cannot change if your heart isn't in it. If you do not truly desire it, it does not take, so to speak. The body rejects it, and the subject dies. Believe me, I know. I tell every single person this beforehand, and still, people have gone through with it, unsure. And then they die. And it is a horrible death. Nasty and unclean. You just saw John. Did he look unwell?"

Ebner only stared at him.

"No, he looks healthy," said Fuchs. "Because it is what he wanted. I presented him with a clear set of choices, and he picked what he thought was most attractive. He chose this path, Mr. Graves. And you still can, as well."

"Stop asking," said Ebner. "Because my answer isn't changing. Not for you, and not for John, and not for anyone else. I'm keeping my land, and I'm keeping my humanity."

"But why?" asked Fuchs. "Because you are used to your lonely, sad life? Because you fear happiness? Because you desperately crave death, out of some misbegotten desire to reunite with your beloved William?"

Ebner stared at him, frozen.

"You cannot keep secrets from me, Mr. Graves," said Fuchs.

"Did John—"

"No, John did not tell me. He doesn't know, still, and he never will, unless you tell him," said Fuchs. "He believes you were friends, like most do."

"Then how?"

"Do you know how sensitive my senses are?" asked Fuchs. "It's overwhelming, at first. And takes centuries to truly understand what you're perceiving. At first, it's just data. So much of it. You get lost in it. But once you pick it apart, you can learn almost anything about someone without them even speaking. Just now, for instance, when I mentioned his name. Your heartbeat accelerated. Your pupils dilated. Your smell—my god, if you could smell it. Those things don't happen to friends, not even the best of friends. This is love, Mr. Graves. And while I don't begrudge your grief, I do believe waiting to die is one of the most foolish things a man can do."

"I'll see him again," said Ebner.

"No, you won't," said Fuchs, his hollow eyes staring deep

into Ebner. "There is nothing after this life, Mr. Graves. No heaven, no hell, no limbo, no paradise, no pain. There is only nothing. There will be no reunion, no salvation, no reward or punishment. Darkness is all that waits for you. What am I offering you is an eternity in the light."

Ebner only stared back into the hollow eyes, searching desperately for a lie, but he couldn't find it, saw only the truth, Fuchs himself said it. He never lied.

"So please, Mr. Graves, reconsider," said Fuchs. "I don't want us to be enemies. I want us to be friends. I want a future for you in Fleet. Alongside John. With enough money and power to get whatever your heart desires."

"You can't give me what I want," said Ebner.

"You're trying my patience," said Fuchs. "I have a strict timetable for the development of Fleet, and I've already ran over my previous two deadlines, which is not typical. If we cannot come to an agreement, I will have to move forward without your compliance."

"What does that mean?" asked Ebner.

Fuchs shook his head and sighed, a deep lonely breath. "Why do you think I make these offers? Why do you think I've come to you, twice now, and have taken all these steps to try and make peace with you, to make a more than generous offer multiple times?"

Ebner stared, not answering.

"Do you think it's because I need your consent?" asked Fuchs. The question hung in the air. "Because I don't. You keep calling me and my children names. Animal, freak, monster. You won't call us human. That's okay, because we're not. We're something more. We're smarter, faster, stronger. We are immortal, aside from an errant shotgun blast, I suppose. Do you know what I've accomplished in my life? More than someone like you can imagine. And believe me, my project would be a terrible plan if it was reliant on a bunch of rednecks and farmers to agree to my offers. Most do, of course, because why wouldn't they? But there are always men like you, Mr. Graves. Stubborn. Obstinate. Stupid. Most of them eventually acquiesce. Some don't. But that does not stop me."

The world seemed to freeze around them. The breeze stopped blowing. The errant sounds of birds and traffic faded away. Everything froze.

"I did not order the deaths of Mr. Snyder or Mr. Stevens, but do not take that for sympathy. I expect my children to control themselves. Their deaths are meaningless to me. And yours would be as well, Mr. Graves. I make my offers because I pity you and your kind. So weak, so short lived. Like mayflies. You blink, come into existence, and then vanish before you've realized the world exists. So I try and provide some comfort to you in that short time, provided you stay out of my way. The best and brightest, I welcome into my flock. You would be welcome, Mr. Graves. All you have to do is accept."

Ebner stared at him, directly into his hollow, blackened gaze. "No."

Fuchs narrowed his eyes quickly, a small gesture.

"You have until tomorrow, Mr. Graves," said Fuchs, the world spinning back up to speed, birds chirping, the warm, dry breeze blowing past them. "Like I said, I have a timetable to keep to. Take the night, and reconsider. And please, let John tell his mother the news. I think that's only fair."

"I'm not changing my mind," said Ebner.

"That's really too bad," said Fuchs. "Because tomorrow I demonstrate a display of force."

And then he walked inside John's shop, leaving Ebner on the sidewalk, alone. Ebner's chest was tight, and full of pain, and rage, and sadness, and he wanted to charge back into the shop and scream, and yell with barbarous anger.

But he didn't. It would do nothing.

He went home, and he called Joanna. Called her because he didn't think he could handle seeing her face when he delivered the news.

She handled it well, considering, a great silence from her end after he told her. Her first words back were what he expected.

"We need to kill Fuchs, Ebner."

18

Ebner spent the rest of the day doing chores around his house. Mostly though, he just thought. He thought about about what Fuchs had said, about Joanna, about John.

He thought about vampires. If they killed Fuchs, what would happen? He knew in some movies that it would revert all the other vampires back to normal. Ebner didn't know if that was true. He believed what he had seen, and what Fuchs had told him. He knew a shotgun had killed the monster outside his house. Would it kill Fuchs?

He didn't know.

He would say that he considered Fuchs' offer. That he stopped and held it in his mind, what it meant for the town, and for him. And maybe Fuchs wasn't lying, and all he said was true.

But Ebner didn't consider it. He couldn't. The thought of it made him sick. It was about control. Fuchs would control Fleet. Fuchs would control John, and him, and everything that Ebner ever knew. And Ebner didn't know if he could stop him, but being complicit in it wasn't in his DNA. He'd sooner die, Heaven or Hell or nothing.

Would his shotgun kill Fuchs?

He didn't know, but he got a call from the alarm company, telling him that the alert went off at Morris' store the next day.

"Should I alert the local police?" asked the dispatcher, probably sitting hundreds of miles away in some call center.

"No," said Ebner. "Probably a false alarm. I'll go turn it off."

It wasn't a false alarm. Ebner realized what Fuchs had meant by a display of force. Fuchs was going to take Morris' store from him. That wouldn't do.

Ebner got dressed and jumped in the truck and drove into town.

He left the shotgun at home. Hadn't come to that. Not yet.

He brought the old axe handle, though. Several trucks were parked out in front of Morris' store, and the door was wide open, propped open. Two men walked out carrying boxes of screws, some of Morris' stock. Ebner hadn't touched the place since Morris had died.

He got out of the truck, holding the cudgel strong in one hand. He looked for sunscreen dripping off them, but he didn't see it. Didn't matter at this point. He'd scared off Fuchs' ghouls before, and he could do it again.

"What the fuck do you think you're doing?" asked Ebner.

The two men looked at him, confused.

"We're emptying the store," said the first.

"It's my store," said Ebner. "That's breaking and entering, robbery, trespassing."

"Don't know what you're talking about," said the other. "This is Mr. Fuchs' store. Told us to clear it out. Renovations start tomorrow."

Ebner advanced on them. "Drop that shit and clear out, or you'll be pissing blood for a week." He raised the handle.

A voice yelled out from behind him.

"Drop it, Ebner," said Sheriff Hicks. "Nice and slow."

Ebner turned to see Hicks and two deputies standing behind their cars, guns drawn, aimed at him. They were parked in the middle of Main Street. The street was empty except for them. He hadn't heard them pull up.

Of course you didn't. They were probably parked at the side street, waiting for you to show up. This is a trap, Ebner.

"You got here awfully quick, Sheriff," said Ebner. "Did the alarm company call you? I told them not to bother."

"Drop that club, Ebner," said Hicks. "I'm not asking."

Ebner brought it down to waist level, but he didn't drop it. "This store is mine, Bart. Morris left it to me. After Fuchs had him killed."

"Mr. Fuchs says otherwise," said Hicks. His pistol was still aimed at Ebner. "And I told you drop that club."

"You can fucking shoot me in the street, Bart," said Ebner. "But I've had this axe handle for three decades, and today ain't the day I'm losing it."

"Ebner—"

"How much is he paying you, Hicks?" asked Ebner. "How much? I know he's got a house already picked out for you in Sunny Meadows."

Hicks stared back, not saying a word.

"Is it money at all?" asked Ebner. "Maybe he promised he'd turn you, change you into one of those things after everything's gone through. Make sure you and the wife are in their little club." Hicks stared back, his face plain. "No surprise, no reaction. You have to be in on it, then. Shouldn't be surprised, I guess. Never could trust a cop around here, and you're no better than any of them. But you ain't the town. How many people are you gonna point guns at, letting that bastard have his way?"

"It's for the best, Ebner," said Hicks. "Fleet was dying. Now it's not."

"You're in league with a monster, Bart," said Ebner. "And I won't stand for it." Ebner advanced on Hicks, walking toward his car.

Hicks shook his pistol at him. "Stay where you are, Ebner. I swear to God, I will shoot you."

"You'll have to, you Judas," said Ebner. "Shoot me. If someone is going to put me down, at least it's someone local." Ebner still walked, only ten feet from the car.

"I'm not joking, you stupid old bastard," said Hicks. "I don't want to hurt you. You could have made this easy—"

"You think I've ever done things the easy way?" asked Ebner. Five feet now. The wooden handle was hard in his hands, and he squeezed it, waiting for the shot to come. If this was the way he'd go, so be it. An honest death.

"He's right, you know," said Fuchs, from behind him. Ebner stopped, turned. "It didn't have to come to this. Sheriff, please lower your weapon. I don't want Mr. Graves harmed."

Hicks lowered his pistol, and he nodded to his deputies

to do the same. Ebner barely noticed it, his eyes on Fuchs.

"You planned this," said Ebner.

Fuchs sighed. "Of course, Mr. Graves," said Fuchs. "If you're not going to accept my offer, please go home."

"Fuck off," said Ebner. "That's my property."

"Possession is nine-tenths of the law," said Fuchs. "Are you going to take it back from me with that club?"

"If I have to," said Ebner. "You don't own this town. You don't own these people."

Fuchs stared at him. "I'm not going to argue again with you, Mr. Graves. I'm past that, at this point. I made my case. So instead, a demonstration for you." Fuchs raised his right hand and snapped. Ebner stared, confused. And then he saw movement out of the corner of his eye. The street had been empty, but a door opened from the small office across the way. A few people walked out, none Ebner recognized. More doors, opened from nearby businesses. The sandwich shop. The mechanics two doors down. From out of alleys, from side streets, from the next street over. People marched in, standing all around them, massing in a circle around Ebner and Fuchs. More and more piled in, and Ebner looked, hoping that maybe they were all newcomers, all residents of Sunny Meadows.

But they weren't.

He recognized many of them, friends or children or grandchildren of people he knew, people he trusted, people from Fleet. They poured out, standing dozens deep around them both. More and more added. Ebner hadn't seen this many people on Main Street in years, and they all stood and stared at him.

"I—"

"You are alone, Mr. Graves," said Fuchs. "You are the only one who wants Fleet to remain the way it is. All these people have sided with me. All of them see the writing on the wall. They see the future. You're not just opposing me. You're opposing all of them. There is no changing this. There is no stopping this. Go home, and wait to die. Fleet will live without you. Fleet will build around you."

Fuchs snapped his fingers again, and the crowd dispersed, turning and walking away, back to where they came from. Ebner watched them go, sorrow in his heart. It was a trick, it had to be, all those people, they couldn't—

"Please, Mr. Graves," said Fuchs. "You're holding up progress."

Ebner stared at him, and Fuchs stared back, his eyes hollow, his face bored, empty. Ebner tried to find the discipline and danger in his eyes, tried to summon the same look that had scared Patrick Hart straight. But he couldn't find it. Fuchs remained unimpressed. Ebner walked past him, to his truck, the handle heavy in his hands.

"If I see you in town again, Ebner, I'm going to arrest you," yelled Hicks, but Ebner didn't respond. He got in his truck and drove home.

19

Ebner found himself at Fleet Cemetery again, standing at William's tombstone.

The graveyard was empty except for him, the midday sun beating down on him. A slight breeze blew past.

"What do I do, Will?" asked Ebner, staring at the piece of stone. "What do I do?"

You've got to move on, Ebner.

"I can't do that," said Ebner. The hospital bed stood in the living room of Will and Joanna's house. It was too big for any other place, and so they had converted the room to a full on hospice center for William. Ebner stood next to his bed, looking down at what remained of Will.

Will was a handsome man, his face delicate and soft. He went through phases where he'd grow a beard, to look more masculine. He'd heard people call him "babyface" his whole life, and Ebner understood wanting to escape it.

But Ebner thought it was a crime to cover up that beautiful face with a beard that didn't suit it. Will's eyes were a brilliant green gold, a color that Ebner knew by heart, could summon in his mind at a moment's notice. His hair had been a chestnut brown, and then slowly turned to salt and pepper, and then white, and then nothing at all, after the radiation and the chemo killed it.

Ebner had wanted to shave his head in solidarity, but Will had called him a damn fool. "No use both of us being ugly," he had said.

Ebner looked at William, and he still saw that beautiful face, even if most of it had sloughed away as the cancer and the chemo had eaten away at him. His body was thin and frail and empty. Ebner had carried him to the bathroom, and it felt like carrying the corpse of a bird, fallen from its nest. He weighed nothing, as if the cancer had stolen away everything inside of him. It wasn't the weight of a man. It couldn't be.

Joanna had left them alone, to get groceries. She had said nothing, but it was really just to give them some time. Will was near the end. They both knew it, and Ebner wouldn't get any more chances. This was it.

"You've got a lot of time left," said Will.

"I don't know about that," said Ebner. "The way I feel in the morning—"

"Don't tell me that," said Will. "You've never smoked, and you're still strong as hell, even now. You've still got time. I'm dying."

"Don't say that," said Ebner, looking away. He had told

himself he wouldn't cry, not today. He didn't want to waste his last moments with Will bawling his eyes out.

"Hell, Ebner, it ain't rocket science. Look at me," said Will. "Ain't much left of me. Doesn't matter what I do."

"The doctors said—"

"The doctors want to give me more chemo, more radiation, for what? A 5% chance at living six more months? I'll pass," said Will. "I'd rather go out now, when I haven't lost my mind. I *am* dying. I don't know when, but it'll be soon. And you could live another twenty years."

"You're all I got," said Ebner. "I can't let go, just like that."

"That ain't true," said Will. "I'm just a part, a piece. And you've got to replace me with something else."

"I can't just take a pair of scissors and cut out the parts of me that aren't convenient, Will," said Ebner.

"Don't let my memory keep you stagnant," said Will. "I've done it too much in this life. I don't want to do it after I'm dead, too. I've told the same to John and Joanna. Death is just the next step. I'll be waiting for you, I promise."

Ebner looked at him, tears in his eyes. He hugged Will then, embraced him, and bawled, and Will held him. Ebner didn't have the words.

Ebner stared at the tombstone.

"What do I do? Fuchs has taken control over everything. He's got Morris' store now, even if Morris' will says otherwise. He's got the Sheriff on his side, and how am I supposed to fight that? Fight the whole damn town? Joanna says we should kill him."

A breeze blew past.

"I want to," said Ebner. "More than anything. But when I look into his eyes, I don't see any fear of death. None at all.

Of anything, really. He's not afraid of me, or anything I can do. I tried to hit him. I'm not as fast as I once was, but it did nothing. He moved, so fast, faster than that one that came for me at night. I don't know if we *can* kill him, if there's any weakness to him at all. God knows how old he is, how long he's been around."

"I failed you, Will. He's got John now, under his wing, and even worse, John chose it. Maybe, maybe if I stop Fuchs, John will come to his senses. Maybe that will wipe out that curse. It's all I got left, you know. I can't let it happen. I can't lose John too. He's all—"

He's all that's left of you.

Ebner's breath caught in his throat, and the tears came then, hot, pouring down his face, and he stood there, crying, his cheeks wet, sobbing, his lungs burning. He cried until all his tears were gone.

When there was nothing left, he grabbed a handkerchief from a back pocket and wiped his face and blew his nose, and then again. He felt better, if only to let it out.

"Joanna is right. We have to do something about it. Even if we fail. We have to try. I'll talk to her. See if we can plan something. She's my only ally now. And you, I guess. I'll get John back, Will. I promise."

Ebner walked over and touched the tombstone, softly, and then left, stopping to do the same for Morris.

Joanna could help him. Together, they could find Fuchs' weakness and strike. They could stop him.

Ebner drove to her house, full of energy again. He felt a shred of hope, something he'd lost since he'd found out the truth about John. He pulled up the driveway and parked.

Joanna answered the door after Ebner knocked, her face

full of sadness, those unyielding eyes soft and vulnerable. They looked the same way they had when Will got his diagnosis, when the reality of the world weighed heavy.

"Can I come in?" asked Ebner. Joanna stared at him, mutely. "I want to talk about Fuchs."

"Yeah, sure," said Joanna, moving out of the way, and Ebner walked himself to the kitchen, where business was done. Joanna joined him, her footsteps soft on the wood floor. He sat in the familiar place. Joanna didn't, sitting a seat apart.

"How you holding up?" asked Ebner.

"I'm struggling," said Joanna. She wouldn't look up at Ebner's eyes. "The news about John, about the shop—"

"It's hard," said Ebner. "They took Morris' store, Jo. I went down there, and tried to stop 'em, but Fuchs had the Sheriff run me off. He summoned hundreds of people. Out of nowhere. He's got his hooks deep. We have to do something, stop him. We have to kill him, like you said."

Joanna looked up then, meeting his eyes, and Ebner couldn't find her inside them. He searched, searched for the woman that Will had married, who had never pulled that pin, but she wasn't there. She was gone.

"I'm sorry, Ebner," said Joanna.

"Don't apologize," said Will. "It's hard, I know. I just went and saw Will—"

Joanna cried then, covering her face with her hands. Ebner watched, putting a hand out to her shoulder, trying to comfort her. Her skin was cold.

"Are you okay?" he asked. "Are you sick?"

"I'm sorry, Ebner," said Joanna. "I'm so, so sorry."

"What are you sorry for?" asked Ebner. "It's not your fault. We can fix this."

"There's nothing broken, Ebner," said John, from behind him. Ebner's blood ran cold, and his heart froze.

No, no no no.

Ebner didn't turn to John, only stared at Joanna. She looked again at Ebner, her eyes full of empty sorrow.

"What did you do?" asked Ebner.

"She made a choice, Ebner," said John. "She made the right choice, in the end. She saw the writing on the wall, and she chose the future, instead of the past."

Ebner stared at Joanna for a second longer, and then stood up and turned to face John. He stood in the doorway to the kitchen. He was dressed nicely, in slacks and a button-down shirt.

"Your own mother?" asked Ebner. "What has he done to you?" Ebner felt the rage rise within him, his chest constricting. His fists tightened.

"When will you understand, Ebner?" asked John. "Oskar has just given me an opportunity. And she asked for it, Ebner."

"I don't believe it," said Ebner.

"What you believe doesn't matter," said John. "It is simply the truth."

Ebner turned back to Joanna. "You told me—you said—"

"What are we fighting for, anymore? Why are we doing this, Ebner? Why fight this?" she asked.

"Because I don't want to be no Goddamn bloodsucking monster," said Ebner. He wheeled back to John. "Some creature that feeds on others. You can talk about your health, and your strength, but at the end of the day, you're draining folks for it. And I don't care how you justify it."

John only stared at him. "If you won't join us, you should

leave. Leave, and never come back."

"Would you tell your father that, if he was here?" asked Ebner. "What if he was standing by my side? Because that's where he'd be. He wouldn't be joining Fuchs, standing by a monster. Selling his soul. He'd be fighting it."

John wavered, his eyes looking away for a second, and then back.

"Yes," said John.

Ebner sneered. "You're lying, John."

"He's not here," said John. "He's dead."

Ebner wanted to swing at him. But he wouldn't waste the energy. Not here, not now.

"Does Fuchs live in Sunny Meadows?" asked Ebner.

"Why?" asked John.

"I want to talk to him," said Ebner. "I want to meet with him, now."

"I don't think—"

"I don't care what you think, boy," said Ebner. "My business is with him, not with you. Yes or no."

"Yes," said John, narrowing his eyes.

"Call him, and tell him I'm coming," said Ebner. He didn't wait for an answer, marching out of the house, to his truck.

He didn't go straight to Sunny Meadows, though.

He went home first and grabbed his shotgun.

20

Ebner was at Sunny Meadows in ten minutes. The guards at the gate eyed him.

"Fuchs is expecting me," said Ebner. "Where's his house?"

Ebner saw the derision in their eyes, but they told him. John had called Fuchs, and Fuchs couldn't resist. Of course he couldn't.

Ebner followed the directions. They weren't hard, and they led to a house at the end of a cul-de-sac, the three story model. Fuchs parked his truck and grabbed his shotgun. As he got out, Fuchs left his house and stood on his porch, waiting for him.

"Mr. Graves, I see you've changed your—"

Ebner didn't wait, leveling both barrels at Fuchs and pulling the trigger, the cacophonous sound of the shotgun firing filling the air.

KAPOW. The shot echoed across the sky.

Ebner reloaded the shotgun on reflex, popping open the barrels, plucking out the empty shells and loading new ones. It took him less than five seconds, but he kept his eyes on Fuchs.

The gun had worked on the thing that had come for him in the night. Two barrels of buckshot, and it had burnt away, turned to ash.

But he knew Fuchs was different. He was the master, and the master vampire was always different.

So he watched Fuchs, seeing if he'd get up. Seeing if he could take the punishment. The gun fired, the shot exploding out, smoke filling the air.

It had been fast. Ebner didn't see contact, but Fuchs was gone, and he assumed the shot had landed, knocking Fuchs down, out of sight on the elevated porch.

Ebner reloaded the shotgun and then it was out of his hands and he was hit hard, harder than he'd been hit in his entire life. He hit the ground, the wind knocked out of him. He took a great gasping breath, trying to make sense of what happened. The realization struck him hard.

He dodged it. That fucker dodged it.

And then he realized his shotgun was gone, out of his hands, not laying near him on the ground. A shadow covered his face. Ebner looked up to see Fuchs, the gun in his hands. He had snatched it without Ebner even seeing.

"Oh, Mr. Graves," said Fuchs. "So be it." Fuchs took the barrels of the shotgun in both hands and bent it neatly in half, and then tossed it aside. Ebner struggled with what he saw.

How?

"Did you really think that would work?" asked Fuchs, as he bent down and grabbed Ebner by the throat with one hand, and lifted him into the air. Ebner fought against him, beating at his arm, but it was made from steel. Ebner couldn't breathe, trying to force a breath in, but Fuchs' grip was too strong. Fuchs threw him across his front lawn and Ebner hit the ground heavy, and he felt something inside him crack.

Ebner gasped for air, his heart beating hard. He had cracked a rib, he was pretty sure. He looked up. Fuchs slowly walked toward him, but they weren't alone. A crowd was gathering. All young people, nicely dressed, emerged from the surrounding houses. Surrounding them, just like on Main Street.

Fuchs stood next to Ebner, staring down at him. Everything hurt, and Ebner forced himself to his knees, his back screaming with pain. Every breath sent an electric shock through his nerves.

"No one here is to harm Mr. Graves. None of you lay a finger on him," said Fuchs, looking out at the gathered crowd. His children. "Get up. You came here to fight me. To prove your mettle."

Ebner hurt, but he pushed himself up to his feet, his body aching. He stared at Fuchs, and Fuchs stared back. Ebner squared up and jabbed with a right hand. Fuchs didn't move, letting Ebner hit him.

It was like punching an oak. Ebner felt two knuckles give way, broken or dislocated. Ebner didn't know. Fuchs punched him once, a movement Ebner didn't see, only felt, an incredible flare of pain in his face, and he felt his nose break with a small crack. Darkness encroached on his vision temporarily, but then the light came back.

He fell, the force too great to resist, his hips, knees, legs all tired.

"I'm centuries old, Mr. Graves," said Fuchs, still standing. "We grow stronger as we age. Do you think a shotgun would kill me? Or that you could beat me in a fistfight?"

Ebner spat out blood, his nose bleeding down into his mouth.

"I don't have anything else," said Ebner. "It was worth a shot."

"Such a poet," said Fuchs, who reached down and picked up Ebner again, holding him by the throat. "You are made of tissue paper, Mr. Graves. I could tear you apart with my bare hands without even a thought. I could rip out your spine without effort."

Fuchs held him there with one arm, even as Ebner struggled, and then he hit him, once, twice, three times on the left side of his body, and Ebner felt another rib crack. He could barely breathe, and each impact rattled him. Fuchs would kill him. Fuchs would kill him.

"This is only a small fraction of my power," said Fuchs. "And I haven't even transformed. This is my mercy." He let go of Ebner's throat and punched him again, on the chin, and Ebner fell, and his lights went out for a moment, the darkness taking over. His vision came back a second later. Ragged breaths came into his lungs, each breath a scatter-shot of agony. God knows how many ribs were broken.

Ebner remembered John. He remembered the look of sadness on Joanna's face and William as he laid dying. Ebner pushed himself up, sweat pouring off him, every part of his body screaming with pain. Blood oozed from his mouth. He'd bit his tongue with Fuchs' last punch. He spit it out onto Fuchs' lawn.

Ebner looked over into the eyes of the assembled crowd. They'd grown in number, hundreds of them all watching as Fuchs dismantled him. They stared, but Ebner found no pity, no sympathy in their faces.

"What are you looking for?" asked Fuchs. "Help? You won't find it. I've offered it to you, multiple times, and every single time, you have declined. More than that, you have spit in my face. And yet still, here I am, offering. Join us, Mr. Graves. Sell your property to me, and in return, all the wealth you'll ever need, for a life that will never end. Your injuries will heal in moments. Your health will be guaranteed. All you have to do is accept."

"No," said Ebner, gasping, every breath agony. He stood up, despite everything in his body telling him not to. "Never. I'll die first."

Fuchs stared at him, and then smiled.

"Is that a fact?" asked Fuchs, and then he was on Ebner in an instant, grabbing him by the throat again, holding him still while he hit him, over and over. Never hard enough to kill him, never enough to knock him unconscious.

Like tissue paper, he had said.

Ebner only felt the impacts, and the pain, as Fuchs peppered his face with punches, over and over. His brain rattled in his skull, and Fuchs let go, and Ebner fell, tumbling to the ground. His head vibrated with pain, his entire face a bruise. His jaw ached. His mouth filled with blood, but he couldn't spit, only let it drool out, so he could still breathe past broken ribs. His vision was fading now. He had absorbed too much punishment.

"Finish it," muttered Ebner. "You'll have to kill me."

Fuchs smiled and kneeled next to him, and spoke so only Ebner could hear. He put a gentle hand to Ebner's aching chin and lifted to look into his eyes. "I *will not* let you die, Mr. Graves. I will live to see you become one of us. You will never see your beloved again. You will live *forever.*"

Ebner couldn't focus on his face, darkness overtaking him, encroaching and then receding, like waves on the shore. Fuchs stared at him for a moment longer, and then stood up.

"Someone get the doctor," said Fuchs. "Take Mr. Graves to see him. Ensure he lives." Fuchs disappeared again, and Ebner's vision faded away. He felt a multitude of hands lift him up, easily, like he was light as a feather, like the corpse of a bird, with empty bones.

They moved him, and everything went to black. He had only visions then, small glimpses of the world, his body moving without him present.

Lights were on him, blinding him.

"He got the hell beat out of him," said a voice.

"Patch him up," said another. "Keep him alive."

"I'll do my best," said the first.

Then there was more pain, abstract, on his ribs, his hand, his face. It brought him back to consciousness, hands touching from beyond the blinding light above him.

"Where am I?" asked Ebner.

"I'm fixing you," said the voice. "At least what I can. Relax. Rest."

"Don't touch me," said Ebner, but he couldn't find the strength to move.

"Relax," said the voice. "This will help." And then there was a prick in his arm, and the darkness returned.

And it stayed, for a while.

A different voice woke him next.

"You alive?" asked the voice.

Ebner tried to speak, but his jaw and throat were filled with broken glass. All that came out was the sound of shatter. He blinked his eyes open, but they resisted. They were heavy. Everything hurt.

"What was that?" asked the voice, again. It sounded familiar, somehow.

"I said—yes, I'm alive," said Ebner, forcing the words out in a distinct croak, his voice harsh. It hurt like hell to talk, but he could do it. He forced his eyes open, and all he saw was a striking bright red halo, the sun shining through the person who stood above him.

"You look like hell warmed over," said the voice. "And you sound like you gargled with gasoline."

Ebner stopped for a moment, and glanced around, realized that he was lying on his front porch, on the wooden swing. His back was stiff. Everything was stiff. He looked up again, let his eyes adjust, and he recognized the person who stood above him.

"Well, I fought a vampire, and he beat the shit out of me, Ms. Wraithwhite," said Ebner.

"That's good to hear," she said, extending him a hand. He took it, and she pulled him up to a sitting position.

"What? That I'm still alive?" asked Ebner.

"No, that it's a vampire," said Ms. Wraithwhite. "I didn't come out to Bumfuck, Texas for another false alarm."

21

"You got my message," said Ebner.

"Yeah," said Ana. "I think I've called a dozen times."

"Sorry," said Ebner. It still hurt to breathe. "I've been busy."

Ebner sat on his porch and looked around, trying to get his bearings. The sun shone bright, high in the sky. His face felt like raw steak. He tentatively reached to it, finding bandages covering parts. His nose burned with every breath.

"What day is it?" asked Ebner. "I've been out for a while."

"It's Wednesday," said Ana.

"Jesus," said Ebner. "I was out for two days."

"What the fuck did he do to you?"

"He beat the shit out of me in front of his whole brood," said Ebner. "And then sent me to his doctor. I think."

"He really has a hate-on for you," said Ana. Ebner glanced at her. She looked like her video on the internet, with her bright red hair tied back in a ponytail, her pale skin glowing. She wore a white blouse with brown riding pants and black knee-high boots. The green amulet hung around her neck. It seemed brighter than his memory.

"I don't know what that means," said Ebner, staring at her.

"Most vampires just kill people who get in their way," said Ana. "Strange he made sure you lived."

"He wants me to be one of them," said Ebner. "Wants to break me down. Rub my face in it."

"Pride," said Ana. "Why doesn't he just turn you?"

"He told me you can't change someone against their will," said Ebner. "Said it'll kill 'em. Thought you were an expert."

"I'm still working on my vampire dossier," said Ana. "That's why I'm here."

"I guess I'm your guinea pig," said Ebner. "Could have used one of your videos before Fuchs came to town."

"Fuchs?" asked Ana. "The vampire?"

"Oskar Fuchs," said Ebner. "Built Sunny Meadows, the development down the road. Then started buying up property around town. Did more than that. Started turning people into vampires. I realized it all way too late. They got everyone."

"Not you, though," said Ana. She looked into his eyes, and didn't break eye contact.

"I guess not," said Ebner. "Although I don't know what I can do. I've tried everything, and got the shit kicked out of me for it."

Ana stared at him in silence for a moment, eyeing him

up.

"Do you believe in monsters, Mr. Graves?" asked Ana.

"Just call me Ebner," he said. "And I don't know, to answer your question. I believe in what I see. And I've seen those ghouls do shit that's inhuman. So I believe in that."

"Ghouls are something else," said Ana.

"What?"

"Don't worry about it," said Ana. "Most people think my internet presence is an elaborate joke. A gimmick, to earn clicks. Monsters are real, Ebner. They exist, and I hunt them. And I kill them, if necessary."

"What are we talking about?" asked Ebner. "Vampires, obviously. But what else. I saw your channel. Demons, werewolves. All of them are real?"

"Yes," said Ana. "To varying extents. Usually not like in the books or movies. But recognizable. Men that transform into beasts. Evil creatures from other places."

"And you've killed them?" asked Ebner.

"Yes," said Ana. "When necessary."

"But not always?" asked Ebner.

"Sometimes they are innocuous," said Ana. "Sometimes they just want to be left alone, away from everything else. They are an accident, or a remnant. They don't want to hurt anyone. In those cases, I do my best to help."

"And in the others?"

"When they are malicious, or malignant, I eliminate them. By any means necessary."

"They can die," said Ebner. "The bloodsuckers."

"You've killed them?" asked Ana.

"One," said Ebner.

"How?"

"With my shotgun," said Ebner. "Two barrels in the chest. It turned to ash in front of my eyes."

"Regular shot?" asked Ana.

"Buckshot," said Ebner. "But nothing else special about it."

"What time of day?" asked Ana.

"Night. After midnight," said Ebner.

"So they can die in the dark," said Ana. "I wasn't sure."

"That one did," said Ebner. "I don't know about the rest. But the shotgun failed me against Fuchs. He dodged the shot."

"And he beat you in daylight?" asked Ana.

"They wear sunscreen," said Ebner. "Seems to protect them from the sun. But Fuchs—"

"What?"

"Fuchs is invincible. He's fast, and strong, and that's just in human form."

"What do they look like when they transform?" asked Ana.

"Their face splits open, and there's a tendril in there, with a little mouth on the end," said Ebner. "It latches onto the victim, drains their blood. I saw their hands change too, elongate, get sharper. I don't know what else they do. That's all I've seen."

"I think they're capable of more," said Ana. "I've gotten reports of more drastic transformations, when necessary. But it's all hearsay."

"Fuchs is very old. He said they get stronger as they age," said Ebner.

"My suspicion is that a lot of them are hiding in plain sight," said Ana. "Among the rich and powerful. They accrue wealth over generations, passing it down to themselves. They fake their death, and take the inheritance as one of their children."

"Fuchs wants to turn the town into a feeding tube," said Ebner. "Make it a support system for his children in Sunny Meadows."

"I doubt this is the first time he's done it," said Ana.

"Do you know—"

"Do I know what?" asked Ana.

"Do you know if we kill Fuchs, if the rest of them, if his children—"

"If they'll go back to normal?" asked Ana.

"Yeah," said Ebner.

"Who did he turn?" asked Ana.

"A man named John. He was like—like a son to me. His mom too. He turned them both."

"I don't know," said Ana. "Again, it's never like it is in movies. Maybe they'll go back to normal. Maybe they'll die. Or maybe they'll just stay vampires. Hard to say."

"What do you know?"

"I know they're not magic," said Ana. "Holy water and crosses do nothing. God can't hurt them."

"He told me God isn't real," said Ebner. "Told me there's nothing but darkness after we die."

"But sunlight does weaken them. UV light in particular. Makes them more vulnerable. Slows them down."

"Doesn't help us if they wear sunscreen all the time," said Ebner.

"There're ways around it," said Ana.

"I'm sure there are," said Ebner. "But I'm not in much shape to do anything right now. I can barely move."

"Let's get you inside," said Ana. She offered him a hand, and Ebner took it, and then she put his arm around her, half carrying him. It hurt like hell, but she supported him as they went inside. The door was unlocked. They walked to the couch and Ebner fell into it, his ribs screaming in pain.

"Ugh," he grunted. "I'm fucking falling apart."

Ana walked into the kitchen and came back with two glasses of water and immediately chugged her entire glass.

"Goddamn," said Ebner.

"It's important to stay hydrated," she said. "Your house isn't very secure. Only two doors in, but lots of windows open to the outside. No attic or basement to fall back to."

"When I bought the place I wasn't thinking about defending against hordes of vampires. There is the root cellar. It's underneath the floorboards in the kitchen. You think they're going to attack us?"

"They will," said Ana. "And the cellar might prove useful."

"What do you mean, they will?" asked Ebner. "When?"

"After we strike," said Ana. "Fuchs will order an attack. Try to kill me, certainly. You, I don't know. He wants you alive."

"Has anyone seen you in town yet?" asked Ebner.

"I don't think so," said Ana. "I came straight here."

"They'll know soon enough," said Ebner. "You want to attack them?"

"Of course," said Ana. "We have to strike now, and show them we're not afraid. Take away their strength, one piece at a time."

"There's only two of us," said Ebner. "And I'm a broken down old man. My ribs won't be healed for weeks, if not months. I can barely move."

Ana looked at him again.

"I'm sorry, I am, but I'd only slow you down right now," said Ebner.

"Do you believe in magic, Ebner?" asked Ana.

"Magic?" asked Ebner. "Like David Copperfield? Dr. Strange?"

"Dr. Strange is closer," said Ana.

"I told you. I believe what I see," said Ebner. "Why? You got some cards up your sleeve?"

"No," said Ana. She sat down in Ebner's recliner. "I am not a monster hunter by accident, Ebner."

"I assumed you weren't," said Ebner. "Doesn't seem like a trade you just fall into."

"It was no accident," said Ana. "It runs in my blood."

"I've never heard of any monster hunter families," said Ebner. "But I haven't traveled a lot."

"My father was a hunter, and my grandfather, and so on and so forth. Six generations back, we have hunted creatures from the dark, and sent them back when necessary."

"Can I ask—how exactly have you and your family made a living at that?" asked Ebner.

"They were nobility," said Ana. "Their wealth was assured."

"Rich folk," said Ebner. "Bored rich folk."

"At first," said Ana. "I'm not rich, Ebner. I wouldn't have a YouTube channel if I was rich. Hunting monsters doesn't exactly pay well nowadays. I've gotten lucky with a wealthy benefactor a couple times, but those are few and far between."

"Then why do you do it?" asked Ebner.

"This," said Ana, grabbing the amulet that hung around her neck, and holding it out away from her. It seemed to become brighter at her touch. Ebner stared at it. The amulet was green, matching Ana's eyes, and seemed quite plain. Gold bordered the green, and then Ebner stared at it, and it became brighter under his sight, and he saw the green move, saw figures arise from within it, wielding swords, crossbows, and rifles. They swirled inside the field of green, saw great battles with creatures unimaginable, shapes and sizes never documented. They swirled and mixed and bled inside the green and then Ana covered it with the palm of her hand.

Ebner blinked, able to focus again.

"Don't look for too long," said Ana. "It's not good for you."

"What is that?" asked Ebner.

"It's the Wraithwhite Phylactery," said Ana. "Found by William Wraithwhite hundreds of years ago. It is bound to our family, protecting us from evil and in return, we destroy all abominations."

"I saw—I saw things in there."

"My ancestors."

"Your family is in there?"

"Once we die, the phylactery claims our spirits," said Ana. "And it's passed down to the eldest child."

"And you just carry them around in there?" asked Ebner.

"The amulet harnesses their energy to—to affect the world, let's say," said Ana. "To weaken my enemies. To strengthen me and my allies. To destroy the indestructible."

Ebner stared at her. "What's the catch?"

"I must hunt," said Ana. "It knows me. It knows my feelings and my thoughts, and it must be used to hunt. We must hunt together, until it is over, or I am dead."

"So you don't have much of a social life," asked Ebner.

"I squeeze it in when I can," said Ana. "But no, not really."

"Are you saying that thing can heal me?" asked Ebner.

"It can help," said Ana. "If it feels you're properly motivated."

"That son of a bitch has taken my town, killed my friends, and turned the only people I love into monsters," said Ebner. "How much more motivated do I have to be?"

"You must declare fealty," said Ana.

"Like a knight?" asked Ebner.

"Something like that," said Ana. "And once your task is over, it will release you."

Ebner stared at her hand, holding the amulet. "That sounds like I'm trading one master for another."

"Do you want your son back?" asked Ana.

"He's not actually—"

"Do you want him back?" asked Ana. "Do you want to kill Fuchs? Do you want to cleanse your town?"

Ebner took a deep breath. "More than anything."

"Swear fealty. The phylactery will heal your wounds, and together we will reclaim your town."

"Do I need to get down on my knees or something?" asked Ebner.

"Don't be ridiculous," said Ana. "You only have to say it, and mean it."

Ebner took another deep breath, and nodded at her. Ana uncovered the amulet, and the swirling green came back into view.

"I swear fealty, until Fuchs is dead and the vampires afflicting Fleet are dead or gone." The amulet glowed brighter still, and the swirling mists inside the green became wilder and wilder, and Ebner found himself lost in it. He saw a future, saw death, and violence, and an end.

And then the amulet was still, and they were both sitting in his living room again.

"Is that it?" asked Ebner. "My ribs still hurt like hell."

"It's not instantaneous," said Ana. "Give it a couple days."

"What are we going to do in the meantime?" asked Ebner.

"We're going to get ready," said Ana. "We'll plan. And then we'll kill some fucking vampires."

22

"You still awake?"

Ebner's eyes fluttered open to Will's voice in the dark. Will's arm wrapped around his chest, a reassuring presence.

"Yeah," said Ebner. "I'm still here."

"I've got to get going soon," said Will.

"Stay for a little bit longer," said Ebner. "It's not even 3 yet."

"I know," said Will. "But I can't stay forever."

The night was quiet, the ceiling fan in Ebner's bedroom blowing down on them. The crickets chirped outside.

"Believe me, I know," said Ebner.

"What does that mean?" asked Will.

"What do you mean?" asked Ebner. "I know you have to leave. It's been the same way forever."

"We don't have to do this," said Will.

"What are you on about?" asked Ebner. "I wasn't complaining."

"You always wanted more," said Will. "You were never happy with us."

"What?" asked Ebner.

This isn't right. This isn't right.

Will's voice lowered in the dark, a rasping growl, a voice from some other place. "You hated me for it. Deep down inside, you hated me."

"Will—" Will's arm tightened around Ebner, and he tried to force it away but it was too strong, too tight, and he was trapped—

"You hated me, and you let John go because of it," said Will, his arm changing shape, mutating around him, and Ebner wanted to scream but nothing came out. "You let him become one of those things—"

"I tried, Will, I tried—"

The light snapped on and Ebner saw Will transform in front of him, his face splitting open, the grotesque maw opening, the tendril reaching for his flesh, draining him. Ebner still heard Will's voice.

"You failed him, Ebner. You failed Fleet. You failed *me*."

The tendril shot out of Will's monstrous visage and reached for him, and Will held him in place, and it would kill him, and he would fail, fail everyone—

Something shook him, and the tendril still reached—

"Ebner!" a voice said, and shook him, and he opened his eyes. Ana stood over him, her strong hand on his shoulder. "Wake up, Ebner."

Ebner blinked, sunlight filling his room. "What time is

it?" he asked, his heart beating hard in his chest.

"It's past nine," said Ana. "You were yelling in your sleep."

Ebner breathed, trying to slow his heart. "I had a nightmare. What was I saying?"

"You kept saying 'Will', over and over again," said Ebner. "Saying 'Will, I'm sorry.'".

"I overslept," said Ebner.

"You needed the sleep," said Ana. "To heal. How you feeling?"

Ebner stretched, testing his ribs. The pain was still there, but distant. It didn't hurt to breathe anymore.

"Much better," said Ebner. "I guess that thing works."

Ana leaned back against his dresser, and Ebner sat up in bed, rubbing his eyes. His heart rate had slowed. He could think again.

"Who's Will?" asked Ana. Ebner eyed her.

"John's father," said Ebner. "Was my best friend. He—he passed last year."

"The amulet can cause vivid dreams," said Ana. "And nightmares."

"I've been having them lately anyway," said Ebner. "Memories of the past." He breathed in. "We need to get John back."

Ana only stared, thinking. "That'll be hard, especially if he's one of them."

"The rest of them can rot, for all I care," said Ebner. "But not John. We need to try. *I* need to try."

"We don't even know if it'll matter," said Ana. "Even if we can get Fuchs. I don't know if it'll change anything. It might be irreversible."

"I have to try," said Ebner, staring at her.

"Didn't he choose to change?" asked Ana, looking right back.

Ebner took a deep breath. "If we can get him away from Fuchs, I can talk sense into him. I know I can. I have the words."

"I don't—"

"It will upset Fuchs, too," said Ebner. "He's using John against me. It might fluster him."

"There's merit to that," said Ana. "Let's take it one step at a time. I got in touch with a local contact. He's bringing us weapons and supplies."

"How local?" asked Ebner.

"Six hour drive. Louisiana," said Ana. "Helped me with a zombie problem. I trust him."

"Zombies?" asked Ebner.

"Don't ask," said Ana. "But I'm putting together a shopping list for him. He'll be here tomorrow."

"Well, let me get dressed," said Ebner.

They reconvened in the kitchen. Ana had taken over the table, covering it with a giant piece of paper, where she had drawn a rough map of Fleet and the surrounding area.

"Obviously, our final target is Fuchs," said Ana. "And Sunny Meadows. His stronghold. But we can't start with a direct frontal attack."

"What do you suggest?" asked Ebner.

"Guerrilla strikes," said Ana. "Starting with the Sheriff's office."

"Attacking the Sheriff?" asked Ebner. "I get it, but attacking the law will only get hell rained down on us."

"I don't intend to leave any survivors or witnesses, Ebner," said Ana. "We take them out completely. As long as

Fuchs has local law enforcement on his side, we are at a disadvantage. We have to take it out. Vampires operate undercover. They only reveal themselves when absolutely necessary. We can't be subtle. We have to force him out."

"I don't know if they've been changed or not," said Ebner. "That goes for a lot of people. Some of them still might be human."

"The phylactery will know," said Ana. "But we'll have to face the fact that we might have to fight humans. Fuchs knows using them as cannon fodder might make us hesitate."

"I don't want to kill good people caught up in this," said Ebner.

"We might not have a choice," said Ana.

"And what about the law?" asked Ebner.

"Vampires disappear after they're dead, right?" asked Ana. "Plausible deniability. And I know a few people, if it comes to that."

"If you know a few people, why don't you call them now?"

"It doesn't work like that," said Ana. "They can't get involved directly."

Ebner waved her off. "Fine. But I don't want to kill people if we don't need to."

"I agree," said Ana. "I kill monsters."

"Then what do we need?" asked Ebner.

"Firepower," said Ana. "Direct firepower. Assault rifles, shotguns. UV lights, as big as possible, and something to power them. We have to be ready for attacks at night. Because they will come."

"You know of anything else they're weak to?" asked Ebner. "Silver? Garlic?"

"I was thinking about that," said Ana. "Obviously, they wear sunscreen for a reason. Sunlight hurts them. UV light hurts them. But why?"

"I don't know," said Ebner. "I'm not much of scientist."

"UV light causes the human body to create Vitamin D," said Ana. "I think that whenever they've changed into a vampire, they can't process it anymore, for whatever reason."

"You're trying to tell me that excess vitamins hurts them?" asked Ebner.

"Vitamin D toxicity is a thing," said Ana. "But I think we should get some, and try and weaponize it."

"I guess it's worth a shot," said Ebner. "We need a cage."

"For John?" asked Ana.

"Yes," said Ebner. He stepped twice, on the floorboards. "Root cellar is right beneath us. We make it a cage. Attach it to the foundation. Don't think John could escape. I doubt he's as strong as Fuchs."

"That sounds like a lot of work," said Ana.

"I can weld," said Ebner. "A few hours work."

"That's good to know," said Ana. "Because we might need it. We've got to strengthen the defenses of the house, too."

"What can this guy get us?" asked Ebner. "Anything?"

"I mean, pretty much," said Ana. "He has back channel military contacts. Things will fall off the truck if he needs them."

"Alright," said Ebner. "I got some ideas, then."

*

The supplies arrived the next day, Ana's friend showing up with a big flatbed truck, the back covered in a tarp.

"This is Louis," said Ana. "Louis, Ebner. Ebner, Louis."

Ebner reached out his hand to the massive man with the light brown skin, his head shaved bald. He smiled and took Ebner's hand, and nodding to him.

"Louis doesn't talk," said Ana. "Get everything we need?"

Louis nodded at her and winked and uncovered the back of the truck. Crates were stacked on it, and a forklift was attached to the back.

"Were you seen?" asked Ana.

Louis shrugged at that. Hard to say. Louis climbed up into the forklift and unloaded crates. Most were small, but a few were big, the wood creaking as the weight transferred to the forklift. Within an hour, the truck was empty, and Louis was already gone again, back on the road, with a hug for Ana and another handshake for Ebner.

"He means business," said Ebner. "Why can't he talk?"

"Someone cut out his tongue along the way," said Ana.

"Jesus hell," said Ebner.

"He liked to talk," said Ana. "Not so much anymore."

Ebner stared around at the piles of crates. "Jesus, it's a lot. What's the plan?"

"First, we build. Then we attack. Unpack and organize the guns. Modify the house. And then we work on your truck."

"Sounds like a plan," said Ebner. It had been two days of sleep, and he felt as good as new. His ribs and face had healed completely. Better than new, honestly. Hadn't felt this healthy in years.

The next couple days were a blur, as Ebner and Ana worked from dawn to dusk, fortifying the house, building, planning, preparing. It felt good, frankly, to be working toward something again. Ebner slept soundly.

"Surprised they haven't attacked yet," said Ebner. He'd kept his head up and eyes open, waiting for Fuchs to send someone to attack, to investigate what they were doing. He had to be watching, right?

"Why would they?" asked Ana. They sat at the kitchen table, eating dinner. Both of them had worked all day. The completed cage sat beneath their feet. All the windows were barred, the doors lined with heavy iron gates. They would finish the truck tomorrow.

"I don't know," said Ebner. "Seems prudent to me."

"You're not a threat, Ebner," said Ana. "That's the advantage we have. It's the advantage I normally have against these things. They always have had the power. Always have had the advantage. They've never even really had to try in their lives. I don't know if Fuchs knows I'm here, but even if he does, I don't think it would change anything. What could *you* possibly do to *him*? You're just some stubborn bumpkin. He's seen a version of you a thousand times in his life and has forgotten all of them. He's never felt vulnerable."

"Not anymore," said Ebner. "Motherfucker's in for a rude awakening."

"You say that now," said Ana. "Be careful. It can swing the other way just as fast. Never underestimate your enemy. Always press the advantage."

"Don't you worry about that," said Ebner. "If I can get Fuchs under my boot heel, I won't be afraid to step down."

*

"You ready?" asked Ana.

"I guess so," said Ebner. Normally Ebner could control his nerves, but not today. His stomach burned with anxiety.

"It will all go fast after this," said Ana. "No turning back."

"I'm already past that," said Ebner. "We got everything we need."

"Triple checked," said Ana.

"Let's do it," said Ebner.

It was just past nine, right when the Sheriff's office opened to the public, and before everyone went out on patrol. Would get everyone in one fell swoop.

They rode in Ana's jeep, with Ebner's truck parked next to the house, covered in tarps. They would need it later. The open top of the jeep would suit their purposes today. Ana drove down Ebner's long driveway. Ebner rode next to her. It had been a week since he'd been into town, since the day where everything fell apart.

The town felt alien now as they cruised through it. More of the local shops had closed down, and construction happened everywhere. Ebner saw a few local staples still standing, but even more empty storefronts were either already open or would open soon.

It had been only a week.

"I can barely recognize it," said Ebner. "Right at the stop sign. Past the library."

Ana said nothing. Ebner looked at her eyes, and they were hard. She looked different now, with something changed in her. Her eyes were greener, and the amulet swirled fast, a tornado around her neck.

Ana parked on the street across from the Sheriff's office, the small building Ebner had gone into not that long ago. His heart was pounding, and his hands were damp with sweat. He wiped them off on his pants, rubbing them together slowly, trying to breathe.

"You ready?" asked Ana.

"What does your amulet say?" asked Ebner. "Any humans in there?"

Ana touched a hand to the green vortex, her eyes looking over to the building. It took only a moment, and then she let go.

"No," she said, her voice something else. "Only abominations. Four of them, including the Sheriff."

Ebner eyed the amulet. But after it had healed him, he had no reason to distrust its power. The Sheriff had already betrayed him and the town. In for a penny, in for a pound.

"No holding back," said Ebner, climbing into the back, pulling open the crate in the backseat. He took out what it contained. It was heavy. He had practiced holding and aiming it back at his house, but practice was different from live fire. He knew that.

"No," said Ana. She flipped open her coat, revealing two holsters under her arms, both with massive revolvers. She stood on the backside of the Jeep, drawing both guns. "Fire when ready."

Ebner stood up, his upper body protruding out the top of the vehicle. He pulled the bazooka onto his shoulder, lining up the sight with his eye. He aimed for the front door of the building.

He took a deep breath and fired.

23

The bazooka fired as Ebner pulled the trigger; the rocket left the tube with a THOOMP. It roared through the air, across the street, and into the Sheriff's office.

Ebner remembered the explosions from Vietnam. He had gotten used to them, so long ago.

The rocket flew into the building, exploding with a cacophonous roar, all the windows blowing out, the ground shaking from the explosion. Car alarms in the area immediately went off. The sound, the fury stunned Ebner for a moment, but only a moment. They weren't done.

They couldn't assume that one rocket was enough. Ebner ducked down and grabbed the assault rifle from the back of the Jeep, and then climbed down, Ana already marching toward the building. Smoke poured from the windows and front door. Fire burned inside.

The street was empty. Reinforcements would likely be there soon. They couldn't dawdle. The blast would have either killed or wounded everyone inside, and perhaps stunned them, but if they indeed all had been changed, they would recover quickly.

Ebner and Ana posted up outside the front door, now gone, one on each side. Ana nodded at Ebner and he grabbed the IED that hung off his belt. It was a modified grenade, a grenade encased in a small jar of powder. The powder was crushed Vitamin D. He pulled the pin and tossed it inside. They both covered their ears, and seconds later, the building shook again as the grenade exploded. It would be a test case for Ana's theory. Would it weaken the vampires?

They found out quickly. Ana led the way in, her revolvers out. Ebner followed, rifle to his shoulder.

The interior had been destroyed, the furniture in pieces and burning. The deputy at the desk had been obliterated by the rocket, but as they entered his body was already burning up, the self-destruct button triggering. Ana swept the room, looking for the other three.

The remains of a desk shifted to their left, and Ana pivoted, kicking the wood aside and firing three shots, loud in the building, POW POW POW. Her hand cannons kicked as she fired into the chest of the vampire that struggled underneath the desk. Another deputy. His arms had been mangled in the blasts, but they were already healing. Ana's bullets stopped that, and he went still.

"Two more," said Ana. A shifting noise came from their left, and another deputy pushed his way out of his office, the wall collapsing in on him. He looked unhurt, and he had already begun to change, his face splitting open, his arms elongating, his fingers sharpening.

Ebner didn't think, only turned and fired, one burst, two bursts, three bursts from his assault rifle. It kicked against his shoulder, BAPBAPBAP, three times, and all nine rounds hit the deputy in the chest, a percussive thudding following each hit. It made a noise, the creature's death echoing through its chest, and then it slumped over.

"You bastard," said Hicks, standing up from behind his desk. "You don't stand a chance." He charged at Ebner, even as Ana turned to fire. He moved quickly, but not imperceptibly. Ebner still couldn't pivot in time, and Hicks hit him, knocking him down. Hicks was on top of him, trying to overpower him, but Ebner found himself holding his ground.

"What did you do to us?" asked Hicks. "Where's my power? I can't—I can't transform."

"Live by the sword, die by the sword," said Ana, and she stabbed Hicks in the throat, plunging her hunting knife deep into his flesh, and then kicked him off Ebner as he struggled, dark crimson blood pouring out of him. Hicks thrashed in the wreckage, trying to hold his throat closed. Ana stood over him and fired once, twice into his head, and Hicks died. Within thirty seconds, his body burned, just as the three deputies had.

"Let's go," said Ana, pulling up Ebner. They left. They parked only three minutes ago, and they jumped back into the Jeep. Ana peeled off.

The anxiety that had plagued Ebner earlier was gone, as they drove back toward his home. Ana drove back a different route, going around Main Street. They pulled into the driveway, less than twenty minutes after they had left.

"Step one, accomplished," said Ana. "But we can't let them react."

"They'll know it was us," said Ebner.

"That's why you'll call John now," said Ana. "And invite him over."

*

There was a knock at the door within half an hour. Ebner answered it, opening the iron gate inside and looking out at John through the screen door.

Ebner paused, studying his face. He tried to find something familiar in it, anything recognizable of the John Ebner had known for John's entire life.

John looked back, confused and impatient. Ebner thought he saw something, for a moment, but it vanished again, just as quick.

He had to try.

"May I come in?" asked John.

"Sure, John," said Ebner. "Come on in. We can talk in the kitchen."

"I see you've made some changes to the house," said John, casually striding through the living room and into the kitchen. Ana stood in the corner, waiting, still wearing her pistols. John froze when he saw her.

"Who's she?" asked John.

"She's a friend," said Ebner. John paused, took a breath, and sat down anyway.

"Is she the reason all of this is happening now?" asked John. "I thought we had a truce, Ebner—"

"Fuchs beating the shit out of me is not a truce, John," said Ebner. "You're an occupying force. You should have expected resistance."

"You tried to kill him, Ebner," said John. "And you have killed four men, including Sheriff Hicks."

"They weren't men, anymore, John," said Ebner. "Fuchs said that to me himself. Told me he wasn't a man. I expect that means the same for all his children. You included. I don't feel bad when I kill a mosquito."

John shook his head and sighed. "Why do want to talk to me, Ebner?"

"I want to make you an offer, John," said Ebner.

"I'm not interested—"

"Shut your fucking mouth," said Ebner, steel in his voice. He had found it again, and John listened. "I helped raise you, and you will listen to me, even if you have to swallow your whole fucking tongue." Ebner paused. "I'm making you an offer, John. To you, and your mom as well, if she wants it. You're the reason she turned in the first place. The offer is to help me kill Fuchs. Join me and Ana. Help us stop him."

John stared at him with cold eyes. "That's your offer? What do I get in return?"

"My forgiveness, John. That's what you get. I'll forgive you for how you've helped him take over our town. I'll forgive you for selling out your father's name. I'll forgive you. And after we've cleaned up Fleet, and gotten Fuchs out of there, everything will be back to normal."

John stared, shook his head again. "Are you out of your mind? There is no normal to go back to. Normal left a long time ago."

Ebner didn't answer. He just stared.

"And I don't want your forgiveness, Ebner. I don't need it. I feel no guilt in what I've done."

Ebner exhaled, through his nose, a small breath of resignation. He glanced once at Ana, and then back at John.

"What was that?" asked John. "Did you expect me to take your offer? It's much too late for that Ebner. It was too late a year ago, when Dad died. The ship has sailed. Dad is dead, and Fleet is dead. Or it was, until Oskar came to town. And now it's alive again, revived. A place where people can live and not just survive, but thrive."

"Is that before or after you've fed on them?" asked Ebner.

"I was hoping you'd come to your senses," said John. "That you had finally seen the light. But it's clear you haven't. And if you think you're scaring me, you're not. I don't know who she is, but just because she's heeled doesn't mean anything. You got the Sheriff by surprise, but you can't do that with me—"

Ebner glanced at Ana again, and then nodded. She drew her pistol and fired, the sound rattling the windows in the small kitchen. Ebner's ears rang. The shot hit the salt shaker, the small plastic container exploding, sending white powder all over the room. It covered both Ebner and John. Ebner sat there for a moment, making sure it had gotten to John. Making sure it had gotten *inside* John. John stared back, confused.

"She's not even a good shot," said John. "But I would just dodge it anyway. I'm stronger than both of you put together, and faster than your eye can see—"

Ebner punched him then, as hard as he could, a sucker punch across the temple. Ebner had hoped it would have knocked him out, but it didn't, only knocking John down, Ebner's fist aching. It was better than when he had broken his knuckles on Fuchs. John fell to the kitchen floor, stunned. Ebner jumped on top of him, holding him down as well as he could, trying to get control of John's arms.

John struggled, and confusion showed on his face.

"What did you to me?" asked John, struggling. He was stronger than John even before he turned, but Ebner had gotten the drop on him. Ana had already bolted to the center of the room, pushing the kitchen table and chairs aside, pulling up floorboards quickly. Within ten seconds the root cellar was exposed, now an iron cage, only the floor of the cellar untouched.

Ana threw it open, the cold iron slamming onto the floor.

"Help," said Ebner. John struggled, and would overpower him again in a second. But then Ana was there, grabbing his other arm, and then Ebner put his entire weight on his chest, and Ana had her knife to his throat.

"Stop fighting, or you're dead," said Ana.

"You won't kill me," said John.

"I'm not him," said Ana. "I've already told him you're a lost cause. So stop—fighting." John stared up into her bright green eyes and stopped struggling.

"Good boy," she said. "Now get down in the hole." Ebner rolled off of him, and Ana grabbed his wrist. She pulled him to his feet, never letting the knife off his throat. He stared at her as he walked down the stairs, into the cage. Ebner waited for him to bolt, but John knew he had lost, and Ana slammed the iron cage shut and then locked the door.

"What are you doing, Ebner?" asked John. "This changes nothing. I will escape."

"No, you won't," said Ebner. "We've got a secret weapon. Turns off your power. A regular dose will keep you down there. We coated the walls and the floor with the stuff. Every step you take is only dosing you more."

"You can't kill him," said John. "Oskar is invincible, Ebner. Immortal. Forever."

"Nothing's forever, John," said Ebner. "You should know that better than most. You can sit down there and stew for a while. I'll be back in a bit."

Ebner and Ana replaced the floorboards, covering up the cage. Ana walked outside, and Ebner followed her.

"Can't believe that worked," said Ebner.

"I hope you're ready," said Ana. "This was the easy part."

"I'm ready," said Ebner.

"Good," said Ana. "Because at sunset, they'll come for him."

24

They made the final preparations to the house. After all the modifications, it barely resembled the place Ebner had lived most of his life in.

Bars covered every window. The two doors had iron gates installed. Ana sat on the porch, a bundle on her lap. Ebner stared at it, curious, but he didn't ask, not yet. He joined her. He would talk to John again, but he needed some time for the words.

"Generators gassed up?" asked Ana.

"To the brim," said Ebner. "Were five of them really necessary?"

"First thing they'll do is cut the power," said Ana. "I believe in redundancy."

"I'm not arguing," said Ebner. "Just worried, is all. Worried my little house ain't gonna take the beating."

"It'll survive," said Ana. "But again, who knows what they'll do."

"How many, you think?" asked Ebner.

"I don't know," said Ana. "How many did you see in Sunny Meadows?"

"It was a lot," said Ebner. "Couldn't exactly count. Too busy getting my ass kicked. But probably a few hundred. At least. There's a couple hundred houses in there. Not all of them are inhabited."

"He won't send everyone," said Ana. "But he knows we're armed. And we have John."

"He'll want him back," said Ebner. "Don't know if he still wants me alive, though."

"Let's hope he does," said Ana. "It'll slow them down. Give us an advantage."

"Don't think they'll spare you the same," said Ebner. "Though John didn't know you. Guessing Fuchs doesn't either."

"I don't think the monsters talk much amongst themselves," said Ana. "Although, after this—I might start getting a reputation."

She held the bundle in her lap, something long, covered in thick canvas. Her knee bounced.

"Don't think I've seen you antsy," said Ebner.

"Nerves are part of the job," said Ana.

"What's in the canvas?"

"A family heirloom," said Ana. "I only take it out on special occasions."

"Like the amulet?"

"It's a joke, Ebner," said Ana. She pulled the canvas away,

revealing a longsword. "It's my sword. It is a family heirloom, though."

"I guess I shouldn't be surprised," said Ebner. "That's a beautiful weapon."

"Thank you," said Ana. She stood up, holding the sword in one hand with practiced ease. The blade gleamed, the handle wrapped in weathered leather, the hilt made from gold. The blade was three feet long, and it looked at home in Ana's hand. She swung it cleanly, the sword whistling through the air. The amulet brightened as she swung, as did her eyes.

"I assume you're good with it," said Ebner.

"My father trained me," said Ana. "And he was the best there was. I'm not as good as him."

"But—"

"But I am still very good, yes."

"Something special about that sword, isn't there? Your necklace lights up like a campfire when you swing it."

"The phylactery knows when I wield it, when a Wraithwhite wields it. It knows our blood, and it knows our weapons."

"You think it'll come to that? Hand to hand?"

"Yes," said Ana. "You should have a melee weapon ready."

"Give me a second," said Ebner. He stood up, his knees and back feeling strong. That amulet. Whatever it did, it was working.

Ebner walked past his truck, covered in tarps, into the shed, and then came back out a minute later, holding a machete in his hand.

"Will this do?" asked Ebner.

"It looks old," said Ana. "Is it sharp?"

"I keep it honed," said Ebner. "Use it to cut through brush, out on the back forty."

"Have you ever used it in combat?" asked Ana.

"A long time ago," said Ebner.

"Then it's perfect," said Ana. "A blade that is whetted in combat strikes truer than one inexperienced." Her face was cold and serious.

Ebner eyed her, and then her facade broke, a sly grin on her face.

"A joke," said Ana. "It'll do." Ebner swung it, once, twice, through the air. It *would* do.

"I'm going to talk to John for a bit," said Ebner. He was ready. He had the words now. "Could you give us some time?"

"I'll be out here," said Ana. "Come get me when you're through."

Ebner sheathed the machete, the thin layer of leather strapped to his hip. He went inside, pushing open the iron gate, closing it behind him, into the kitchen. John sat in his cage, underneath the floorboards. Ebner heard him breathing.

Ebner grabbed a chair and sat in it, looking down to where John sat.

"How you doing in there, John?" asked Ebner.

John didn't answer, but Ebner still heard him breathe and shift.

"Don't feel like talking?" asked Ebner. "That's alright. You don't have to say a word. But I have some things I need to tell you. Don't know if you want to hear 'em, but that don't rightly matter, not anymore. Probably should have told you a long time ago. At least when Will died. But I didn't. I kept my mouth shut, and my secrets to myself, and hoped that everything would work out, like magic."

Ebner stared at the wooden floorboards. He pictured John down there, the John he couldn't recognize anymore.

Talk, you old fool. Tell him.

"But it didn't work out. Things only got worse. I don't think Will was holding it all together, but it sure seems like it, at times. Keeping everything in line. Maybe he was just the final straw, on a long line of shit. I don't know. But here's the truth, John. Your dad and I were lovers. For most of our adult lives. We kept it secret. Only person who ever knew was Morris, and maybe your mom suspected, but I sure as hell never told her. If Will did, he didn't let me in on it. I don't think you knew, but only you can confirm that."

Ebner waited for something from the cage, but still nothing.

"But there was no man, nothing on Earth I loved more than your father. Loved him enough that I settled for whatever we had here, where he got married, and had a kid, and kept us a secret. I don't know. I've gone back and forth over the years, if it was a good idea or not. If I wasted my time. I might have. But I still loved him. Loved you. Loved Jo, too, maybe because she was the only other person who loved Will like I did."

"Doubt you're finding this pleasant, but I've been carrying it for fifty years, so I think you can handle it. But here, all of this is just to say this."

He paused. "I'm sorry, John."

Ebner took a deep breath and let it out, slowly.

"I'm sorry for keeping you here," said Ebner. "I'm sorry for selling you the shop when the plant closed down. It was your dad's idea, you know. He wanted you close, and I didn't need the shop. My pension and social security is enough for me to live on. He wanted you close. The plant did right by both of us, and we thought it'd do the same for you. But we were wrong, idealistic. Stupid, even. We thought that because it'd always lasted, it would continue to last. Same with this town. But we were wrong. I was wrong. And I could blame it all on Will, but that ain't right either. He can't answer for his part in it, but I can answer for mine, and even after he died, I still wanted you here. You're as close to a son as I'll ever have. And—"

Ebner's voice caught in his chest. He wiped away a tear.

"—And you're all that's left of him," said Ebner. "I told him—I told him before he went, that I'd take care of you. To him, you were always his little boy. No matter how old you were. You're a grown man now, but to him, you were always that little kid, who needed protection, who needed advice. He told me to mentor you, y'know. He told me you listened to me. I wasn't your parents. I could get through to you. If only Will could see us now. Don't think he'd like it, but that son of a bitch shouldn't have died, huh? Left us high and dry."

"I'm sorry, John," said Ebner. "I really am. But Fuchs isn't the answer. Some bloodsucking carpetbagger isn't the answer. I understand your choice. Money, power. They can be mighty attractive. But forever is a long time. Do you know how old Fuchs is?"

No answer from John, still.

"He's centuries old, at least," said Ebner. "And as far as I can tell, this is his life. He travels around, buys up places, and shapes them to his liking. I guess that keeps him busy.

And when he's done, he moves on, and does it again. And again. And I know he's sold you on it. About living forever. About being invincible. But you aren't, clearly. Us two captured you pretty easy. But I get it. You watched your dad waste away to nothing in front of your face. I saw it too. I still—"

Ebner didn't wipe away the tears now, letting himself cry.

"I still think about Will, seeing him like that. Seeing this strong man waste away to a skeleton. It was horrible, a terrible thing that happened to him. But that's life, you know. And that horrible end doesn't take away any of the great things that happened in his life. Death is just a part of it. And nothing we do has much meaning if we have all the time in the world. Fuchs is empty, John. Ain't nothing inside of him. Time has taken it all away. And given enough time, you'll be the same way."

Ebner wiped his face now, staring down at John, sitting somewhere in the cellar.

"So, here's what I'm going to do. I'm going to kill Fuchs, and hopefully that'll change you back, just like in the movies."

"Oskar said that won't do anything," said John, finally, his voice quiet.

"Well, he's a liar, John," said Ebner. "Regardless of what he claims. And I still owe him for Morris. But either way, I'll let you out of there after he's gone. And you can do whatever you want, including kill me, if it comes to that. Sound fair?"

"What if he kills you?" asked John.

"Might makes right," said Ebner. "Pretty sure that's how he thinks, anyway. I gotta make sure the house is ready for tonight. Thanks for listening."

Ebner waited a moment for an answer, but nothing came. Ebner stood up and went back outside. Ana waited for him.

"How'd it go?" asked Ana.

"Don't rightly know," said Ebner. "Said what I needed to say. We'll see if it works."

"It's dangerous, having him at our backs," said Ana. "If he gets out, we're done for."

"I've thought about it," said Ebner. "But it has to be this way."

"If it comes to that," said Ana. "If he gets out. Could you pull the trigger?"

Ebner took a deep breath and then met her eyes, her bright green eyes.

"If it comes to that, I've already lost."

25

Ebner and Ana spent the rest of the day testing their defenses. They'd had hours until sunset, and it seemed like plenty of time to get everything ready, but soon the sun was setting, and they both retreated inside. There was no more time. They turned off everything inside. The darkness in matched the darkness out.

John was silent, saying nothing to either of them.

The orange glow in the western sky faded slowly, and darkness encroached from the east. As it arrived, so did the noises in the dark.

"They're out there," said Ebner. He whispered to Ana as they waited inside the house. They had moved the furniture aside, or thrown it outside. It would only get in their way. Ebner hadn't seen his house this empty for many years. But they had replaced it with generators, with lights, with racks of weapons and ammo.

"They're testing us," said Ana. "They want us to reveal ourselves before we need to."

"How will we know when to kick on the lights?"

"We wait until they're knocking down the door," said Ana.

They waited.

Ebner held a shotgun, this one pump action. His machete hung off his side. Ana held a single pistol, the other still holstered. Her sword was sheathed on her hip. She crouch walked into the kitchen, seeing if she could see anything outside. Ebner waited in the living room, his eyes looking through the barred window, searching for motion, anything in the darkness.

But he saw nothing.

He only heard the noises, the footsteps, the rustling, the sound of movement through the grass. Tapping on the wooden walls of his shed. His truck was out there, under tarps, integral to the last step, vulnerable to sabotage or destruction, but they had bet on them focusing on the house. Ebner and Ana had John, and that is where they would focus their effort. If Fuchs was out there, he would see it through, but Ebner didn't believe that Fuchs would be here. He wasn't a general that led his troops into battle. He waited at his base.

It didn't get louder, but it got closer, and more numerous. And Ana was right. They made the noise on purpose. They were trying to frighten them. Scare them into making a mistake. Trying to draw their fire so they could isolate and then kill them both.

Or maybe just Ana, and leave him alive, like Fuchs had before. Ebner didn't know and didn't care. He would defend his home to his dying breath.

He felt Ana next to him again.

"They're close now," she said, her voice barely audible. "I'm going to post up in the kitchen. Watch out for friendly fire. On my mark, hit the power."

"Okay," said Ebner, as quiet as he could. He felt her leave, and his hand went to the jury-rigged power switch near the wall. Ana had handled all the wiring, with lengths of cords duct taped to surfaces. Ebner had never been a good electrician, always half afraid of frying himself or someone else.

The noises on the outside of the house multiplied. It sounded like they were surrounded, the creatures everywhere. Would they transform? Would they still be wearing sunscreen, nullifying their advantage?

Ebner didn't know, but the sound got to him. They were out there, moving, waiting, and soon they'd attack. His guts roiled. He remembered John, down there in the cage. They'd come for him. Ebner had to protect him. It was his only chance.

The noise was louder now, and he crouched next to the window in the living room, over where the couch used to sit, and he swore they were right on the other side, and he waited for them to punch through the glass and rip the iron bars away from the house, and jump in and attack—

"Now!" shouted Ana, and Ebner hit the switch, and the area around his house was lit like the noonday sun hit it, powerful flood lights filling the area with UV light. Ebner looked out the window, his shotgun ready, and he saw them. They had mounted dozens of lights to the roof, stacked on top of each other. Both to see in the dark and to bombard them with UV, hoping to nullify some of their monstrous advantages.

They were like legion.

Hundreds of the creatures stood outside, dozens deep, all of them transformed, their faces grotesque and split open, their arms and legs changed and hardened. They screamed at the sudden light, all at once, some shielding their eyes, and their eyes that weren't eyes, and they screamed, an unholy sound, whatever their mouth was now screeching, filling the night air with a terrible cacophony. Ebner froze for a moment.

Ana's voice broke him free again.

"Fire!" yelled Ana, and Ebner didn't stand on ceremony. He rose and fired with his shotgun at the first creature he saw, standing only a few feet from the window. The glass shattered and the creature fell, and Ebner pumped and fired again, each blast knocking a creature down, hopefully killing it, but Ebner didn't stop to check, firing over and over again.

Ana fired as well, booming blasts from her revolvers echoing through the house. The creatures had been stunned momentarily, but now they charged the house, charging the windows and doors. Ebner continued to fire. The creature's arms were pushing through the frame, trying to get to him, and he shot into the mass, repeatedly, until his shotgun was empty. He tossed it aside and grabbed another, racking shot after shot. Each blast roared in the small living room, and the mass of creatures thinned as they ran from the window, looking for another way in.

Glass shattered from his bedroom, and Ebner ran there.

They had pushed the mattress up against the newly installed bars, and Ebner pointed the shotgun around the bed and through the bars, blind firing into the creatures there. They needed to keep them out as long as possible. Ana had said they would take out the power first, but it still—

The lights turned off then.

"Generators, Ebner!" yelled Ana, her revolvers booming periodically. He ran through the house, the bedroom window forgotten. He raced through the darkness, knowing the layout of his house intimately. They had routed the generators to a single switch, and he went to it, pressing it on. They were top of the line, and ran quietly. The lights outside the house kicked on again, but it wasn't as bright as before. He heard the steps on the roof then, and then the sound of lights breaking as they crashed to the ground.

"They're destroying the lights!" yelled Ebner.

"Keep them out!" yelled Ana back, and Ebner fired more shots outside through the living room window as creatures scampered through his sight. They were avoiding the windows, waiting for the lights to be extinguished. Ebner had fewer and fewer targets, and there were more and more footsteps on the rooftop. The lights went out, one by one, crashing to the ground, being ripped from the rooftop. Soon they were in darkness again.

Ebner didn't wait for Ana this time, running over to the final switch as he heard more of the vampires struggling at the iron bars. They wrenched and pulled, and eventually they'd get in.

He hit the switch, and the interior of the house was bright as day, UV lamps nestled in every spare corner blasting the house with light. Ebner saw the creatures again as they struggled at the window, and he fired again and again, racking his shotgun over and over until he was out of ammo. He grabbed another shotgun off the rack, and turned to fire at the window when the iron gate at the front door fell inward. The gate itself was still together, but the mounts had broken away.

"They're in!" yelled Ebner, and turned to fire into the choke point. He killed three before they entered. Ebner pumped and fired, falling back into the doorway to the kitchen. The vampires were slowed as they walked through the UV light, and Ebner fired again and again, more and more creatures pouring into the house. He felt Ana behind him.

"Down, Ebner," she said, and he crouched as she shot her guns above him, deafening him as she gunned down creature after creature. The iron gate at the back door groaned and then was ripped outward.

"Fuck," she said. "Hold this door." She turned, holstered her pistols and drew her sword, swinging it with a speed Ebner didn't realize was possible. He turned, standing again, firing his shotgun into the oncoming waves. They were slowed by the UV light, but still, they moved fast. They grabbed at the generators and the lights, knocking through their defenses, and soon the living room only had the red emergency light, but Ebner still fired in the red mass of creatures as they rushed him.

Ebner fired a final time and then pulled his machete, swinging at the grasping arms, blood flying, and then they had him, lifting him and throwing him across the room. He flew into a bank of lights and they shattered behind him, and his back screamed with pain. He fell to the floor. Ana had held the back door, her sword slicing through limbs and necks. Ebner couldn't believe it, but the creatures were pulling at the floorboards now. They sensed John's presence, and they were clawing at the iron gate set into the cellar, a handful of vampires ripping at the gate, pulling at the iron. It creaked as they used all the strength they had.

Ana realized them behind her and backed her way in front of Ebner as he climbed to his feet. His back had been cut open from the broken lights, and he felt blood drip down his back. The remaining vampires filled the kitchen, ripping at the iron gate, destroying what remained of the generators. Only the red emergency light remained. Ana and Ebner held out their weapons, ready to defend themselves.

With all the UV lights out, the creatures would be at full strength soon, if they weren't already. Ebner watched as they wrenched the iron gate from its hinges. They weren't as strong as Fuchs, but they were still strong. They extended arms down into the cellar and pulled John out. The transformed creatures surrounded him, but John still looked himself. He glanced around in the red, and saw Ana and Ebner in the corner.

He locked eyes with Ebner, with Ebner's unyielding eyes, and Ebner saw something, something he recognized.

"You take the left, I'll take the right," murmured Ana, and then they charged, and they were fast. Ebner swung his machete as hard as he could as they charged in, and Ana did the same, her sword chopping through them, but soon they were caught up in the arms of the creatures, and the vampires held them, their tendrils reaching to feed.

One approached his face, and he held his breath, and closed his eyes, waiting for it to latch on, to drain him of everything. He would see Will again.

But it never came, and then there was a great crashing noise, as a vampire was pulled up into the air and thrown into the wall. Ebner's arms were free and he swung his machete hard, cutting away the tendril, a terrible screech emitting from the vampire he cut it from. Another vampire was pulled back and thrown, and Ana swung her sword.

The dozens and dozens of creatures had been thinned down now, and Ebner now saw what he had recognized in John's eyes.

John had transformed himself, and moved like a blur, grabbing the other creatures and swinging them through the air, into ground and ceiling and walls. He had freed them, and was using his monstrous claws to finish the other creatures off as they were stunned. The few remaining vampires were confused, and Ana and Ebner took advantage, chopping them down. Ana's amulet glowed emerald in the dark, and as the vampires fell they burnt in the red, disappearing into ash.

Ana cut through the last vampire, separating its head from its body, and it fell, and then burnt away. The three of them waited, but no more attacked. Ana held her sword ready, staring at John, still transformed into his hideous form. Ebner stared as well, but then wiped the blood from his machete on his pants leg before sheathing it.

His back ached, but he was otherwise unharmed. John stood there, his body heaving from exertion, and then he transformed back, his flesh sickeningly melding into his normal appearance. His face was his again, and he stared at Ana, and then Ebner.

"I accept your apology, Ebner," he said, and then collapsed to the floor.

26

Ana got one generator running, giving them light, at least enough. Ebner kneeled next to John, whose chest heaved, his body human again.

"I haven't fed in days," said John. "We can't go that long."

"There's no survivors," said Ana. "Lot of ash, but no survivors."

"He must have sent half of the brood," said John. "There's still the other half, though." He looked into Ebner's eyes. "I'm sorry, Ebner. This is all my fault."

"That's not true," said Ebner. "You're standing with me at the end, that's all that matters. You turned the tide."

"As long as Oskar is standing, we can't win," said John. "You have no idea. His plans. I've only seen a little, but he's been doing this for years. There's hundreds of these communities. He wants to—"

"He wants to conquer," said Ebner. "I know. You gonna make it?"

"Yeah," said John. "I can go a little longer. I'll just be a bit slow."

"We can use you," said Ana.

"I don't know if I can transform again," said John. "It takes a lot of energy."

"You don't need to transform," said Ana. "You just need to pull a trigger."

"I can do that," said John. "What's the plan?"

Ebner looked at his watch, under the light of the floodlights. It was still hours until dawn.

"We've got some time to regroup," said Ebner. "And rest. Ana, will you look at my back?"

Ana did, bandaging what she could.

"It won't kill you," said Ana. "It'll just hurt like hell."

"Can't your necklace do something about it?" asked Ebner.

"It doesn't work that fast," said Ana. "And it's having some trouble with John nearby."

"I trust him," said Ebner. "He saved our lives."

"The phylactery doesn't understand that nuance," said Ana. "It sees something inhuman, and it wants it destroyed. It's not the first time."

"I'm John," he said, extending a hand toward Ana. "We haven't been formally introduced."

Ana glanced at his hand for a long moment, and then shook it. "Ana Wraithwhite."

"You think we can get the lights back on outside?" asked Ebner.

"Probably a couple. Enough to see by," said Ana.

Ebner walked through his broken house, the doors gone, the walls filled with stray bullets, the windows broken. They set up some lights outside, and Ebner uncovered the truck, pulling off the tarps. None of the vampires had touched it. Their minds had been on the house, not the surrounding environment.

Ebner revealed the modifications they had done. They had added a roll cage, but that wasn't all.

"What the hell is that?" asked John.

"It's a turret," said Ebner.

"It's a fucking minigun, Ebner," said John.

"Fuchs started a war, John," said Ebner. "And we're going to finish it. You best get used to that thing, because you're going to be firing it."

"Jesus," said John. "Alright." He climbed up into the truck and got behind the trigger, rotating the gun. "I'm guessing I won't get any fire exercises."

"You will," said Ebner. "In about 5 hours, when the sun rises."

The lights on, Ana threw open the shed and started grabbing supplies and throwing them into the back of the truck.

"What's in the boxes?" asked John.

"Explosives," said Ana. "Grenades. Rockets."

"*Who* are you?" asked John.

"I kill monsters," said Ana, with a smirk, and went back to the shed for another box. Ebner helped, and soon the truck was loaded.

"Do you know which houses are occupied?" asked Ana. "In Sunny Meadows?"

"Mostly," said John. "It's not rocket science."

"It will be today," said Ana, patting a box. "How many humans are living in there?"

"None," said John, after a beat. "Everyone's been turned. Oskar won't let you move in until you've been turned."

"Good," said Ebner. "We don't have to worry about killing any people."

"Ebner—" started John, but Ebner cut him off.

"I know," said Ebner. "There's some people in there we know. We won't shoot them if they run." John stared, but then broke his gaze. "It sounds like you were waffling, anyway. Anybody else doing the same?"

"Not that I know of," said John. "Most in Sunny Meadows were true believers."

"That's what I thought," said Ebner.

They went over the plan, backwards and forwards, making sure John knew the score. Ebner eyed him, but he never sensed any hesitance in John. If he was planning on betraying them, he was doing a good job of acting. But they needed the hands if they were going to kill Fuchs. John had already saved their hides once.

The minutes ticked by, and the dark haze of the night glowed from the morning sunlight.

"We should wait until the sun is up completely," said John.

"That's too long," said Ana. "They'll have sunscreened up by then. We need to catch them napping. A little past dawn will have to do."

"I guess you're right," said John. "But Oskar isn't affected as much by it, even without the sunscreen."

"We've got something special for him," said Ebner. "Hope to God it works."

"He knows by now that the attack didn't work," said John. "No one's come back to report."

"You think he's expecting a direct assault?" asked Ebner.

"I doubt it," said John. "But then again, he's been around a long time. He might be ready for anything."

"If he's ready, so be it," said Ebner.

The sun rose, crossing the horizon, illuminating Fleet with early morning light, and the three of them rode. Ebner drove, with John manning the turret, and Ana riding next to him in the bed. Ebner turned out onto the main highway and headed toward Sunny Meadows. He was tired, not sleeping all night, but his heart beat hard in his chest, rattling his rib cage. This was it.

He swung into Sunny Meadows, stopping twenty feet from the entrance gate. The two guards didn't notice him at first, busy staring at their phones.

Ebner yelled back to John. "This is your chance for target practice, John."

John turned the turret toward the guard shack, and Ebner heard the minigun spin up, and the thin whine as it spat out hundreds of rounds in seconds. The two guards noticed far too late, and the minigun ate them up, destroying most of the guard shack and killing them in moments. The gun spun down.

"If they don't know we're here yet, they do now," said Ebner, getting out quickly and opening the gate. It rolled open slowly, and they pulled up.

"Call 'em out, John," said Ana. "And be ready when they charge." Ana pulled up a bazooka, and Ebner cruised down the street as they rained fire on Sunny Meadows. John pointed at the houses, and Ana put bazooka shells into them, the houses exploding, catching on fire.

The vampires had assaulted Ebner's house with furious anger, and now it was their turn, as they picked Sunny Meadows apart. Vampires charged across their manicured front lawns, and John picked them off, the turret making short work of them. It ran out of ammo, and Ana reloaded the big gun before launching a rocket into another house. Ebner drove down the street, a shotgun on the seat next to him, just in case any of them got close.

None did.

Each house was burnt, blown up, or destroyed as they went. The empty houses were left standing.

"They're coming!" yelled Ebner, back to the two of them. He saw the horde streaming out from their houses, running at the truck. John turned the turret, and it spun up to full speed, rounds flitting across the lawn, pavement, road, and through the creatures as they charged. The gun tore them to pieces, and the bodies turned to ash. Ana didn't stop firing the rockets, each of them leveling a house as they went. A long line of burning homes were behind them, and soon the stream of vampires had stopped. The minigun had killed them all.

Ebner continued to drive, heading straight for Fuchs' house, slowly but surely. They took out every home along the way. Most of them had already been emptied, the torrent of vampires running at them already extinguished, but they blew them up all the same. Ana was a machine, firing and then replacing the rocket shells, tossing the empty boxes out the back of the truck.

And then they were there, Fuchs' house in front of them. Ebner parked then, grabbing the shotgun and posting up at his open door, aiming at the house. John turned the turret to the door, waiting on Fuchs to emerge.

Ana didn't wait to see him. She loaded the bazooka and fired, a rocket pluming through the air, directly through a front window and then exploding with a massive sound. Fire burned inside instantly, and Ana fired again through the other window.

"Where is he?" asked Ebner, talking to himself. "You see him?" he asked, louder, yelling back to John and Ana.

"No," yelled John.

Ana didn't answer, but fired a third rocket into the house. It exploded, and smoke poured out of the home.

"Where is—" started Ebner, and then the truck was in the air, knocked up and onto its side. Ebner barely avoided it, the mass of the truck landing on its side next to him. He fell to the ground, and turned to see John and Ana thrown out of the truck, both on the ground. John moved, struggling, but Ana was still.

He reached for his shotgun and then it was ripped from his hands from something he couldn't see. He blinked, and then Fuchs was there, in front of him, holding his shotgun.

Fuchs looked different now. He looked angry. His dark, hollow eyes burned into him. He snapped the shotgun in two and threw the pieces aside. He reached down and grabbed Ebner with a steel hand and pulled him up into the air by the throat, Ebner struggling to breathe.

"Did you think this would be any different?" asked Fuchs, and then he tossed Ebner. Ebner flew and smashed into the pavement, sliding across the road. His body screamed in pain.

Ebner looked up just in time to see Fuchs transform.

27

Fuchs transformed in front of Ebner's eyes, under the morning sun.

He was more than the others.

Fuchs changed, his clothes ripping as his arms grew, his chest ballooning, his head splitting, the flesh tearing into new shapes. Ebner stared, unable to take his eyes away from the new thing that Fuchs was becoming.

His arms elongated, long enough to drag on the ground now, the bones lengthening and stretching, the fingers becoming long claws, and Ebner saw now how myth confused them for bats.

But this thing was not a bat. Fuchs had no wings, his neck extending as well, his face splitting open to reveal a great tendonous maw, a terrible gasping gnaw, reaching for blood, feeling out into the open air. Fuchs face was gone now, but he still saw, because he was on Ebner again in an instant, a long, distended arm picking up Ebner, without effort, high into the air, above Fuchs head.

Ebner struggled, but it was no use, and Fuchs' tendril reached for him. It extended out, through the air, toward Ebner's face, and he battered at the mutated arm that held him, but it did no good, the sheer bone and muscle immovable, invincible.

A great voice rumbled out of Fuchs' body. He had no mouth, but he still spoke.

"YOU HAVE NO IDEA WHAT I AM," he said, the tendril reaching for Ebner. Ebner watched it get closer and closer. It would feed on him in a moment, but Ebner would see it happen. He would not approach his death with eyes closed.

Then something moved quickly through the corner of his vision and hit Fuchs' mutated body, his broad chest smacking with an empty sound, and Fuchs dropped Ebner as he fell backwards from the impact. Ebner crashed to the ground, his hip screaming with pain as he hit the concrete. The wounds on his back had opened up again, and he could feel the blood trickle down his skin.

Fuchs had been knocked backward, but not down, his enormous form still standing. His wide, distended bony chest heaved, but he stood. In front of him was John, who had transformed himself, the milder transformation of Fuchs' children.

"JUDAS," uttered Fuchs, his voice booming from his body like a speaker. "BETRAYER."

John swiped at Fuchs throat with his extended claw-like

hand, but Fuchs moved faster, avoiding it, grabbing him around the torso. John struggled in his grasp, swiping at Fuchs' arm, opening up rivulets in it, black blood streaming from it.

Ebner pushed himself off the ground and ran to Ana, who just now regained consciousness, her eyes unfocused.

"Help him," said Ana. "The rockets." Ebner ran to the truck, pulling open boxes, looking for another bazooka.

John still struggled with Fuchs, Fuchs trying to close his other massive hand around John's head, to crush him. John struggled with it, both of his own hands grasped around Fuchs', pushing it away. He pulled and pulled, and Ebner heard the SNAP as one of Fuchs' mutated fingers broke. He screamed, and then lifted John high into the air before smashing him into the pavement with a sickening thud. John still struggled, and then Fuchs smashed him again, with another sickening thump, and John was limp in his hand, and then Fuchs launched him through the air with incredible strength. John flew and slammed into an intact house, crashing through a window.

"JUDGMENT," uttered Fuchs. Black blood flowed from his broken finger, from his sliced up arm, but the massive shape he had taken seemed invulnerable from real injury. He stepped toward Ebner at the truck.

Ebner found the bazooka and quickly turned, readied, and fired. The rocket left the launcher with a PHOOMP, and flew at the massive target of Fuchs, but then Fuchs simply disappeared, reappearing next to Ebner.

"FOOLISH," said Fuchs, pulling the bazooka from Ebner's grasp and crushing it in a a huge hand. Ebner reached for another box and Fuchs grabbed his left arm, wrapping his distended fingers around it, and then he squeezed.

Ebner's arm erupted in pain, and he heard his bone break with a SNAP. He screamed in pain, and a terrible dark laughter emerged from Fuchs. He held that pressure as Ebner floundered under his grasp.

"TISSUE PAPER," said Fuchs, and then he tossed Ebner through the air, a terrible wrenching pain in his left arm as he hit the ground, his limb hanging useless. Everything hurt, and Ebner felt blood well up in a dozen places. He rolled through the impact. His head was woozy, and his vision swam as he looked up. Fuchs walked over to him, moving slowly. Fuchs had all the time in the world. Ebner tried to shake off the cobwebs. He looked over to the house John had been thrown into, and there was no movement. Ebner hoped he was still alive.

The great voice rumbled out of Fuchs as he strode slowly toward Ebner.

"WHAT DID YOU THINK THIS WOULD ACHIEVE? DID YOU THINK YOU COULD STOP ME? STOP MY GROWTH? THERE IS NO END TO ME, MR. GRAVES. I HAVE GROWN UNENDING FOR CENTURIES, AND I WILL CONTINUE, UNCEASING, INFINITE. THIS DAMAGE IS NOTHING. A SCRATCH TO THE SURFACE."

Ebner glanced, saw Ana moving, crawling to the truck. She was searching through the boxes, upended when it crashed. He forced himself to his knees, and then to his feet. He spat out blood, clearing his throat.

"Oh, go fuck yourself," said Ebner. "You're nothing. All you do is take from good people and pretend like you earned it. Whatever you are—however you want to describe yourself—you're just a monster. And you don't belong here. Try and turn us on ourselves. And I don't care if you're stronger, and faster—you're not better than me. You're nothing but a bloodsucker, a leech that crawled up out of the mud and grew too big."

Fuchs still approached him. Ana had found what she was looking for, hastily loading it near the crashed truck. Ebner drew his machete with his one good arm.

"WHAT DO YOU EXPECT TO DO WITH THAT?" asked Fuchs. "NO HUMAN WEAPON CAN HARM ME." Fuchs looked down on Ebner, his gaping tendril waving in the air.

"I'm going to cut you down to size," said Ebner. "Should have done it the first time I saw you."

Ana brought the rifle to her shoulder, aimed at Fuchs' massive frame, and then fired. The rifle was nearly silent. Ebner didn't hear it. Fuchs may have, but he didn't move, didn't dodge. He didn't see it as a weapon at all, and the dart hit him in his wide back. His head twisted at the impact.

"WHAT WAS THAT?" he asked, unable to reach the dart injecting him.

"It was a guess," said Ebner. "Just a guess."

Nothing happened, and Fuchs stood there, and then laughed, the dark sound emerging from him, booming from him. But Ebner watched. He waited. He ached from a dozen different places in his body. His arm was broken, useless, and his back ached, wet from blood. But the worst pain was in his guts, the tension building, hoping that their guess would work.

And then Fuchs began to change, and Ebner smiled. The transition was slow at first, but Ebner could see it. Fuchs' arms transformed back into normal arms, the broad chest of bone and lean muscle mutated into Fuchs' normal human shape.

Fuchs grunted, unable to speak, his body caught in the transformation.

"Looks like it was a good guess," said Ebner. Ebner watched as Fuchs changed back, and under a minute, he was human again, his clothes in tatters clinging to him.

"What did you do to me?" asked Fuchs.

"Highly concentrated Vitamin D," said Ebner. "Purest we could get. It worked on your kids, but we weren't sure about you. Course, we gave you a lot." Ebner swung his machete, hard as he could, into Fuchs side. Fuchs didn't dodge, didn't intercept the swing, didn't stop Ebner. The machete cut into his side and blood poured from him. Fuchs' face was a mask of shock.

"You look surprised, Fuchs," said Ebner. He swung again into his other side, and Fuchs grunted in pain, blood pouring out. "Must have been a long, long time since someone's hurt you, huh? Must have been a long, long time since you've felt weak."

Ebner reared back and ran him through, the machete stabbed deep in Fuchs' torso. He made a horrible gasping noise, staring at Ebner, shaking his head, mouthing something.

"It must have been a long, long time since you had to confront the reality of dying, huh?" asked Ebner. Ebner pulled out the machete, and Fuchs fell to his knees, clutching his stomach, trying to hold in the blood pouring out from him.

"Pp-pp—please—" said Fuchs, sputtering, blood spitting

from his mouth.

"Begging isn't very becoming of you, Fuchs. You told me Morris asked for mercy. He didn't get none. You won't neither," said Ebner. "Death is just a part of life. Don't you worry. I'm sure the Devil's got a nice place carved out for you in Hell."

Ebner swung the machete hard with his good arm, and cut off Fuchs' head, his body slumping backward. His head tumbled to the pavement.

Ebner watched, and waited, waited for Fuchs to come back, to regenerate, to still live, somehow.

But within a minute his body and head burnt away, turning to ash in front of his face, blowing away on the early morning breeze.

Ana sat near the truck.

John.

Ebner moved as fast as he could to the house John had been launched into. He went in through the open front door, looking for John. He found him, sprawled in the living room, surrounded by shattered glass, the remnants of the window.

"John," said Ebner, slowly kneeling next to him. Every movement hurt. John laid still, but then Ebner saw his chest moving with breath. John's eyes fluttered open, looking up at Ebner.

"Fucking hell," said John.

"You look alright for being smashed into the pavement," said Ebner.

"I trusted him, Ebner," said John. "I trusted him."

"He's dead," said Ebner. "How do you feel?"

"Everything hurts," said John.

"Can you change?" asked Ebner. "Are you still—"

"No," said John. "Whatever it was, he took it with him."

"They are no more," said Ana. The amulet hung quiet around her neck. "The phylactery sees nothing nearby."

John sat up, slowly. "I don't think I'll be dancing anytime soon."

"At least you're alive," said Ebner. He looked to Ana.

"What now?" asked Ebner. "Don't have much experience cleaning up after dead vampires."

"It'll be messy," said Ana. "I'll call a friend. He may be able to help."

28

"What a mess," said Agent Bowman. Ana walked with him through the remains of Sunny Meadows.

"You told me you could clean up anything reasonable," said Ana.

"Reasonable, Ana, reasonable," said Bowman. "You took out a Sheriff's office!"

"They were vampires," said Ana.

"And you're sure about that?" asked Bowman.

"Yes," said Ana. "I've got a dossier on them, now. I can give you what I've got."

"You found a way to stop them?" asked Bowman.

"Yes," said Ana. "Vitamin D."

"Really?" he asked.

"Yes," said Ana. "Makes them vulnerable."

"We have a list," said Bowman. "We suspect others are the same."

"I thought your hands were tied," said Ana. "I thought direct involvement is a big no-no."

"It is," said Bowman. "Quote, 'The United States government can not directly be involved with supernatural entities.' End quote."

"Who said that?" asked Ana.

Bowman just smiled at her.

"But I know it hasn't always been like that," said Ana. "My dad told me stories—"

"Things have changed," said Bowman. "There are more cameras, and more access to information. So we have to be more careful."

"So, can you help me?" asked Ana.

"It is in our best interest to control the flow of information," said Bowman. "So yes. We'll get Fleet squared away. There's already some people on their way. Shouldn't be too bad. I doubt most didn't even know what they were."

Good," said Ana. "Anything you need from me?"

"Well, now that you mention it," said Bowman. "We could use your help."

"Define help," said Ana.

"I told you, we have a list," said Bowman.

"You just said no direct involvement—"

"*We* can't have direct involvement," said Bowman. "Subcontractors are technically allowed."

"You want to hire me?" asked Ana.

"Yes," said Bowman. "We need help domestically, so we're recruiting."

"How much?" asked Ana.

"Whatever you need," said Bowman. "Technically, it's off the books. You don't work for us. Tax free income, and we can provide you with whatever gear you need."

"Do I have to follow orders?" asked Ana.

"There's some flex in that," said Bowman. "We will want input. And you'll have to close your YouTube channel."

"Oh, thank Christ for that," said Ana. "I hate editing videos."

"So you'll do it?" asked Bowman.

"I need to see paperwork," said Ana.

"There won't be any paperwork," said Bowman. "It's all handshake deals."

"Fine, I'll write up my demands," said Ana. "But the first one is I answer only to you."

"I'm not—"

"I know you," said Ana. "I don't want to deal with other people."

Bowman locked at her, his sunglasses hiding his eyes. "Fine," said Bowman. "I'll make it work."

"One other demand," said Ana. "I get an assistant of my choosing."

"Sure," said Bowman. "As long as we vet them."

"Then I'll leave you to it," said Ana. "Send me the list."

Ana walked back to her Jeep and drove off.

*

"How you feeling?" asked Ebner.

"Like warmed over shit," said John.

John laid in the hospital bed. Considering Oskar had smashed him into the pavement, and thrown him into a house, he didn't look too bad. He had started regenerating before Fuchs died and made him human again. It was probably the only reason he was still alive.

He was covered in bandages, and both his legs were broken, but he would live. Ebner sat next to him. They were alone. Jo had been there, but she'd left the room when Ebner arrived.

"You don't look great," said Ebner. "Still better than me, I reckon."

"At least you're walking," said John. "It'll be a while before I'm on my feet again."

"I hear the lawyers said that you own Sunny Meadows now," said Ebner. "Or what's left of it."

"Yeah," said John. "All of Fuchs' holdings in the area fell to me."

"What are you going to do?" asked Ebner.

John looked at him. "I don't know," he said. They sat in silence. The machines attached to John beeped softly. "I'm sorry, Ebner. For my part in this."

"I know," said Ebner.

"I felt like there was no way out," said John. "I could see my whole life, stretched out in front of me, and it scared the living hell out of me. And Dad was gone, and—and I was drowning. And Fuchs was there, with a helping hand."

"You paid your fair share in getting him gone," said Ebner. "You tell your mother?"

John looked at him, Ebner not needing to say what he meant. "No," said John. "That's between you and her."

"Think I should tell her?" asked Ebner.

"I don't know," said John. "I think—I think you should talk to her." He eyed Ebner. "You're leaving, aren't you?"

"That easy to tell?" asked Ebner.

"You hate hospitals, Ebner," said John. "Why else would

you be here besides to say goodbye? Where you headed?"

"I don't know," said Ebner. "Going on the road with Ana. She said she needed some help. Figured it's as good a chance as any."

"She's the real deal, ain't she?" asked John.

"As real as it gets," said Ebner.

"Am I going to see you again?" asked John.

"I don't know," said Ebner. "Doubt I'll be back around, but you never know." Ebner stood. "I'm going to talk to your mom, and then I'm going to head out."

John looked at him, his eyes watery. Ebner hugged him.

"I love you," said John, quietly.

"Love you too," said Ebner. "You do your best. I'll see you down the road."

Ebner let go, and left, and didn't look back. He closed the hospital room door. Joanna sat outside in a chair, her eyes looking down at the floor. She looked up as he approached and sat down next to her.

They sat in silence. Ebner felt an anger inside, for what she did. An anger that she gave up. But it wasn't fair to show it. Wasn't fair to yell, after what had happened. So he just sat there, letting the silence sit. They'd had a lot of time together. They could sit in the quiet just fine.

"Jo—" he started.

"I'm sorry, Ebner," said Joanna. "I'm sorry."

Ebner took a deep breath. "It's alright," said Ebner. "It's all sorted now."

"Don't make what I did right," said Joanna.

"He's your boy, Jo," said Ebner.

"He is," said Joanna. "And he's—" Her breath caught in her throat.

"And he's all you got left." She nodded and pulled a tissue from a pocket, blowing her nose. "I know." He paused and took a breath. "Jo, me and Will—"

He stopped. Joanna had reached over and grabbed his hand, squeezed it, squeezed it hard. Something she had never, ever done. Neither of them were much for casual affection. They had hugged, sure, even held each other bawling after Will's funeral. But she'd never held his hand.

He squeezed back.

"I miss him," he said, finally. "I miss him so much."

"So do I," said Joanna. They sat there, their hands together. Machines beeped faintly in the background. A nurse talked on the phone.

"Jo, I'm leaving," he said. "I'm leaving Fleet. Doubt I'll be back, least while I'm alive."

She nodded. "It's about time," she said.

He nodded. "It is," said Ebner. "Take care of yourself."

She nodded, and squeezed his hand again, harder still, and he squeezed back, and then Ebner stood and left.

*

"I'm leaving, Will," said Ebner.

The sun burned overhead, but the temperature had cooled off a little, a hint of fall approaching. Ebner still sweat, his left arm in a cast, layers of bandages on his side and back. Fleet Cemetery was empty again, except for him. They hadn't had funerals yet for the Sheriff and his deputies. Didn't know if they would. Didn't rightly care, either.

He took a breath. "I don't know what the government is going to do with Fleet. With Fuchs gone, John has control over Sunny Meadows, and a lot of Fleet in general. Don't know if it'll stay that way. I haven't driven back into town, and I don't think I will. There's nothing much left of it I can recognize."

"And maybe that's okay," said Ebner. "Maybe it has to be that way. I think I can finally let go of it." Ebner took a deep breath. "I'm going, Will. And I don't think I'll be back. Maybe they'll bury me here, but I won't be around for that. Fleet doesn't need me anymore. I don't have anything to give it. I killed Fuchs and now it's in John's hands, if he wants it. If he doesn't—well that's okay too. But there ain't nothing left for me here. I've still got some time left, and it's about time I left Texas again. I still love you, that'll never change."

Ebner touched the tombstone and then left the roses. He did the same for Morris. He walked through the Fleet Cemetery, and he didn't look back.

Ana waited for him, her Jeep parked out front. He climbed into the passenger seat.

"You sure about this?" asked Ana.

"Yeah, I'm sure," said Ebner. "*You* sure about this?"

"Yeah," said Ana. "An old cuss like you can be useful, from time to time."

"Listen to you, flatterin'," said Ebner.

"You ready to go?" asked Ana.

"I said my goodbyes," said Ebner. "Let's get the hell out of here. Where we going first?"

Ana eyed him and smirked. "I got a list."

SIGN UP FOR YOUR FREE, EXCLUSIVE NOVEL!

Sign up for Robbie's newsletter! Monthly sneak peeks at upcoming projects, cover teases, and instant access to a free, exclusive novel!

www.robbiedorman.com/newsletter

ACKNOWLEDGEMENTS

Thank you to my wife Kim, for her patience and support. Thank you to my team of beta readers; Andrew, Matt, Megan, and Yousef, for your guidance and help. Thank you, for reading.

ABOUT THE AUTHOR

Robbie Dorman believes in horror. Death Rattle is his eighth novel. When not writing, he's podcasting, playing video games, or petting cats. He lives in Texas with his wife, Kim.

You can follow Robbie on Twitter @robbiedorman

www.ingramcontent.com/pod-product-compliance
Lightning Source LLC
Chambersburg PA
CBHW050255110726
47898CB00007B/2413